Veronica Bennett works part-time as an English lecturer. She began her writing career as a freelance journalist, but soon moved into fiction. *Monkey*, acclaimed by *The Times Educational Supplement* as "an impressively well-written and audacious debut," was her first book. Its theme was suggested by two unrelated tragedies – the suicide of a friend's teenage son as a result of bullying and the riding accident in which the actor Christopher Reeve was paralysed. "Somehow," she says, "the despair of the boy and the courage of the man connected." She has since written *The Boy-free Zone* and *Fish Feet*, and for younger readers *Dandelion and Bobcat*. Veronica Bennett is married to a university professor and has two children.

Books by the same author

The Boy-free Zone

Fish Feet

Dandelion and Bobcat

MONKEY

VERONICA BENNETT

WALKER BOOKS
AND SUBSIDIARIES
LONDON • BOSTON • SYDNEY • AUCKLAND

With sincere thanks to Kath Jones, Clinical Head of Occupational Therapy at Rookwood Hospital, Cardiff, and Robin Christopherson of the Computability Centre, Warwick, for their help, encouragement and patience.

First published 1998 by Walker Books Ltd
87 Vauxhall Walk, London SE11 5HJ

This edition published 2003

2 4 6 8 10 9 7 5 3

This book has been typeset in Sabon

Printed in Great Britain by Cox & Wyman Ltd, Reading, Berkshire

British Library Cataloguing in Publication Data:
a catalogue record for this book
is available from the British Library

ISBN 0-7445-8347-0

www.walkerbooks.co.uk

CONTENTS

DORK

"Go on, Pritchard! Get back to the sewers, where you belong!"

Drowning men are supposed to see their whole life pass before their eyes. But when your head is in the toilet, and you're not sure if you're drowning or not, you don't see *anything*. You don't even open your eyes.

The familiar sound of Gerard Fox's voice in its excited state – high-pitched, nasal, with the hint of a donkey's bray about it – reached Harry's ears as he was hauled backwards by the collar of his blazer. A nervous accomplice, standing guard by the door, was calling, "Brig! Brig!"

But Brig, alias "Brigadier" Gerard, took no notice.

"That's where the rats are, isn't it, Pritchard? That's where people who *rat* on other people have to go, isn't it?"

Harry was aware of the futility of protest. To say he hadn't complained to Mr Mitchell would be about as pointless as the lunatic depravity of ramming someone's head down the toilet bowl with one hand and working the flush with the other. He took a breath, held it and waited for the next ducking.

It came, but there wasn't enough water in the tank for a proper flush. Grunting in frustration, Brig pumped the handle several more times before he was dragged unwillingly away.

"Mitchell's coming! Come on, Brig, leave it."

Harry heard the bell for the start of afternoon lessons ring somewhere very far away. Still kneeling beside the toilet, he folded his arms on the seat – school toilets never seemed to have lids – and waited for his head to stop spinning. As the hiss of Brig's last attempted flush subsided, his forehead sank onto his hands.

"Been swimming, Pritchard?"

"No, sir." Harry lifted his head, but not very far.

"Stand up, boy."

Harry stood up. He felt a bit peculiar, and slumped against the cubicle door. Mr Mitchell looked at him with little, tortoise eyes. "Stand *up*."

With an effort, Harry did so.

"Who did this, Pritchard?"

"Don't know, sir."

"Don't know Fox, I suppose?"

"Who, sir?"

Mr Mitchell shook out a clean pocket handkerchief and handed it to Harry, who began to wipe his streaming face.

"All right, Pritchard, be a hero. But I've got my eye on Fox. The next time he oversteps the line, I'll catch him."

No you won't, thought Harry. He's as slippery as his namesake.

"Thanks, sir," he said, offering Mr Mitchell the handkerchief.

"I'll have it back tomorrow, clean and ironed, please."

"Yes, sir."

"Get along to your class now, then."

"Yes, sir."

"And if you develop the symptoms of cholera or dysentery, you'll let me know, won't you?"

"Yes, sir." Very funny, sir.

Harry was depressed. The toilet incident was the second Gerard Fox encounter he'd had this week. He wouldn't mind if he'd done something to deserve it, but he was the victim of a bully, and the thought made him feel *feeble,* somehow. Like a girl.

And talking of girls, what chance was there that any of them would ever like him – or even notice him – when it was common knowledge that Gerard Fox had singled him out as an easy target? Girls liked boys who were in control. Boys who were in the football team, and scored goals, like Fox himself. Boys who stuck up for younger kids when *they* were being picked on, instead of spending their days skulking around hiding from Fox, and their nights worrying about it.

Even his sister Emma, who was only nine, had noticed.

"You're just not cool, Harry," she'd said accusingly. "You're quite tall, and you've got quite nice hair, but you're just not cool enough for girls to be interested."

His shirt and blazer were damp. As he waited outside Emma's school playground a thin February drizzle began to fall. Miserably he turned up his collar and leaned against the railings, wishing himself many miles away.

Preferably on a different planet. A planet where girls like that dark-haired one, Louise what's-her-name, turned up unexpectedly on the doorstep to ask whether this skirt was too short, or these jeans too tight, or if he was going to Tonio's on Friday night. Most of all, a planet where Gerard Fox, with his sharp features and equally sharp talent for causing Harry misery, didn't exist.

"Harry!"

Emma's full weight on his shoulders pulled him back to earth. She squealed, and jumped down. "Why are you so wet?"

"Even *you* can't be too stupid to see that it's raining."

She looked bewildered. Her face, with its pointed chin and freckle-spattered nose, was very small inside the hood of her new you'll-grow-into-it coat. "But it's only just started, and it's only a *little* rain. You look as if you've been in a thunderstorm."

Harry couldn't look at her any more. His misery suddenly seemed so deep that even his toes were miserable. "Oh, shut up and let's get home. I'm starving."

They set off together down the hill. Harry thought about the tedium of tea and toast with Emma in front of children's TV. He thought about Mum in her blue nurse's uniform, easing her feet out of her shoes. Asking him if he'd remembered to peel the potatoes. Promising him extra money and then forgetting to give it to him. He thought about Dad, getting home later and later every night, more and more exhausted, with a fatter and fatter briefcase.

It seemed that everyone was too busy these days, since Mum had gone back to work and Dad had been promoted, to notice what things were like for him. And although it was nice to have more money, what was the point of new clothes or a flashy bike or a better computer when everyone at school thought he was a total nerd?

In fact, he reflected as they reached the house, he was worse than a nerd. He was a dork. Only yesterday he'd heard Phil Capper, who used to be his mate at primary school, say so.

Emma gathered up Razzle, who was waiting on the doorstep looking damp and unhappy, and took him into the house. "Come on, puss. Teatime. Can he have a saucer of milk?"

"If you get it for him, midget."

When she'd left the kitchen Harry poured

himself a bowl of cornflakes and waited for the kettle to boil. As he crunched, he pondered.

The biggest question of all the big questions racketing round his head kept fighting its way to the front. All right, he was a dork. All right, Brig Fox's anti-Pritchard campaign was so puerile and pointless he ought to be able to deal with it standing on his head. All right, Louise what's-her-name was probably as stuck up as she looked, with ponies on her bedroom wallpaper. But why, given all this self-knowledge, couldn't he find what was needed to un-dork himself? What was it anyway? Bravery? Self-confidence? Plastic surgery?

His brain seemed to wince. Try as he might to stop it, it was filling with a picture he was ashamed to look at. There he was, standing by the door of Miss Drew's classroom, hand poised to knock, heart thundering, sweating. Then the door opened unexpectedly and Louise herself came out. They must have been inches away from each other. He remembered with a twinge that her swinging hair almost touched his shoulder as she turned to close the door. But she'd given him one of her actress looks and walked off with her chin in the air.

Standing damply in the kitchen, three days later, he blushed to think of it. Another opportunity missed. Another embarrassing moment to add to his store of millions. And he hadn't even knocked on the door after all. The encounter with Miss Pony-wallpaper seemed to evaporate his courage. She was a founder member of Miss Drew's Drama

Club, but asking if he could join too would have to wait.

Raucous sounds came from the living room, of a TV cartoon and Emma laughing at it. Harry made the tea and buttered the toast, wondering how old he had been when he grew out of being amused by cartoons about baby animals.

"Here, eat this. And turn down that horrible noise."

"I like it loud. Mum said to get the bread out of the freezer."

"I *know.*" In fact, he'd forgotten.

His fingers were greasy. Digging in the pocket of his blazer, they closed around an unfamiliar bundle. Mr Mitchell's handkerchief, which was supposed to be clean and ironed by tomorrow. He looked down at it with slight panic.

Furtively he filled the washing-up bowl and washed the blue and white checked hanky as thoroughly as he could. Then he wrung it until it was a mass of little creases and spread it on top of the boiler.

Emma came in. "What are you doing? You look guilty."

"Don't talk such rubbish."

"Whose is that hanky?"

"Mine."

She fingered it. "Why is it wet?"

"Why don't you go and watch some more trash?"

"*Animal Crackers* has finished. Have you got the bread out?"

Harry opened the freezer, wondering whether a blow from an ice-hardened loaf would kill a nine-year-old, or just knock her out.

"Dork," she said.

With clenched teeth and superman effort he checked the tension inside him. Emma's opinion didn't matter, after all.

"You're sad, Emma," he told her witheringly. "You're just too sad for me to concern myself with. Why not go and watch some grossly stupid kids' programme and leave me in peace? Would the 'ickle baby do that for big brother?"

She stuck out her tongue and tried to hit him, but he dodged the blow. She began to shout that she hated him and would tell Mum. Harry held her at arm's length, thinking how thin her wrists were, and how red and unattractive her face.

"Go on, then, so that I can hit you and you can whine to Mum about it!" he taunted. "Or try Dad – he's a softer touch, you little toad."

"You'll get into trouble for calling me that! I'll tell Mum!"

"Tell me what?" Mum came into the kitchen and dumped two shopping bags on the floor. "Will you two stop that? My nerves are in pieces today already. Stop it! Do you hear me?"

Emma ran out of the room, dry-eyed. She took the stairs two at a time, then Harry heard the familiar slam of her bedroom door. He knew that Mum would think he had made her cry. He sat down on the kitchen stool, clenched his fists inside his trouser pockets and counted down silently to blast-off.

She didn't mention Emma, though.

"I finished a bit earlier than usual today, so I did a bit of shopping on my way home. Oh, and you remembered to get the bread out." She smiled at him. "You're a good boy, Harry, when you want to be. Goodness, I've still got my hat on!"

Mum was a district nurse, and her uniform always looked to Harry like a cross between a policewoman and an air stewardess. He hated the navy blue pill-box hat even more vigorously than the black lace-up shoes.

"What are you leading up to?" he asked.

She took off the hat and put it down on the work surface. Then she screwed up her eyes and looked at him closely. "Why are your clothes damp?"

He took a step back. "It's raining."

"Didn't you have your coat on?" She came over and felt his forehead. "You look a bit pale, you know. And there are shadows under your eyes. Have you been sleeping all right?"

"Can you say what you want to say and let's get it over with?"

She leaned against the table and folded her arms. "Well, I finished early because the patient I should have seen at four o'clock wasn't in."

"Can't be very ill then," muttered Harry.

"Don't mutter, darling. And would you put those bags on the table for me?"

Harry gave her an exasperated look, and she laughed. "All right, I owe you another twenty pence. I'll never get used to not calling you that, though."

She started to put things in cupboards, talking to

him over her shoulder. "Anyway, I thought this patient, Mr Schofield, was going for his check-up at the hospital tomorrow, but they changed it to this afternoon without telling me. And do you know what?" She paused, a tin of pineapple chunks in her hand. "Driving home, I realized I *missed* talking to him. He really is a very interesting man. You'd like him, you know."

"I doubt it."

"Don't be so cynical. He's not young, but his mind's much sharper than yours or mine. And he has charming manners."

Mum often went on about manners. She put the tin on the shelf and gazed out of the kitchen window for a moment, to an imaginary land where gentlemen held doors open for ladies and children neither bickered during meals nor belched loudly after them.

"It's such a pity. Do you know what he said to me the last time I saw him? He said he doesn't mind the daytime at all – going to the day centre on a Wednesday afternoon, seeing me or one of his other carers, reading, listening to music, looking at his garden – but it's during the evenings that he gets lonely."

Harry was getting bored hearing about an old man he'd never met and wasn't likely to. "What are you leading up to?" he repeated.

"*Well.*" Her bright eyes met his. "In the car just now I had the most brilliant idea. What about *you* going round there a couple of evenings a week, just for an hour or so, to keep him company and talk to him?"

Harry's senses sharpened. *What?*

"He'd love some male company – most of the people he sees are women – and he's just so interesting, Harry, I'm sure you'd—"

"Mum, it's not on, it's just not on. What about my homework?"

"You'd still have time for that. And you haven't got a part-time job like lots of your friends. It would do you good to get out and help someone instead of slouching around in front of the TV all evening."

Desperately, he raked his brain for an excuse. "But if this man – Schofield, or whatever his name is – is so amazing and interesting, why doesn't he go out in the evenings, to the pub or something?"

Mum's excited face softened, like a plumped-up cushion falling in on itself.

"Oh, Harry..." She reached up and ruffled the side of his hair like she used to when she was taller than him. "I must have forgotten to mention it. Mr Schofield is a quadriplegic. He's paralyzed from the neck down."

"He's *what?*"

Harry knew his mouth had dropped open but he couldn't close it.

"His brain's all right, though, darling," added Mum cheerfully, turning back to the cupboard. "Oh no! I've done it again, haven't I? That's another twenty—"

"And I've got to entertain him?" he interrupted. His voice was a squeak. "What am I supposed to do? Juggle? Read fascinating snippets out of the *Guinness Book of Records*? Play Fantasy Football League?"

"You don't even like football, Harry, so don't be stupid."

Harry gulped down three mouthfuls of tea. He was so furious he didn't know how to express it except rudely, and had to stop himself saying something which would end in a punishment. How could Mum, who usually made at least a small attempt to be nice to him, have such a crass idea, and think it so brilliant? And why *him*? If this Schofield bloke was so deprived of male company, couldn't Dad go, or a male nurse, who was used to people in wheelchairs?

"*He* might like football, though," he protested, his voice getting back to normal. "And I've got to do what he wants, haven't I? Like a servant?"

"Harry..." She shut the cupboard door and turned to him. "You wouldn't be a servant. I'm not suggesting that he pays you."

"A slave, then."

"Oh, Harry!" She wasn't annoyed, but her voice was the one she used when he refused to eat something she'd spent three hours cooking. Hurt, but tolerant.

He put down his mug. He couldn't stay in the kitchen a moment longer. He'd go upstairs and plan a campaign. Dad would rescue him. Dad was bound to think the idea was stupid, and convince Mum. Meanwhile, he was too angry to be civil, and had to put some distance between her and himself.

"*Dad* will pay you, though," she said unexpectedly as his hand landed on the doorknob. "You're always complaining you haven't got enough money, aren't you? Well, here's your chance to earn some."

"But Dad doesn't even know about it," he protested. "And when he does—"

"He'll agree to pay you. Hard cash, guaranteed."

"How do you know that?"

"I just do."

"Have you two cooked this up together?"

"Of course not. And don't cheek me. Dad's been thinking for a while that you need something useful to do, which he could pay you for. This is the perfect opportunity."

Harry stepped back from the kitchen door as Emma opened it. She'd forgotten why she had rushed upstairs, and had been painting her toenails.

"How long is it till suppertime? Can I have a chocolate biscuit?"

Mum sat down on the stool and considered her wearily. "You know Daddy doesn't like you putting on nail varnish, little one..."

Emma made what Harry secretly called her boiled fish face – pale, tasteless, dead. "Well, by the time he comes home from work I'll have my socks on again, and he won't see it, will he?"

Mum sighed. "We'll talk about Mr Schofield with Dad later," she said to Harry, as Emma's bare feet and spidery legs scrambled into her lap. "And I expect sensible behaviour."

In the room which was really the spare bedroom but Dad liked to call the den, Harry lay on the carpet and tried to imagine what it would be like not to be able to move. Supposing you sneezed and couldn't wipe your nose? How could you read if you couldn't turn the pages? How could you use the phone or open the front door? What would you do if the smoke alarm went off in the middle of the night?

The truth was, it was unimaginable. And the thought of spending precious hours every week with someone in this unreal, practically unhuman condition not only dismayed but scared him. It would be like looking after a baby, but having to be polite at the same time. It would be like being on trial.

Henry David Pritchard, take the stand. Are you a *nice enough person* to help someone less fortunate than yourself? Or are you so *morally depraved* that you will only do it for money? Can you cope with the *guilt* this man will inflict on you? Objection, Your Honour...

Objection. Well, that seemed futile. Mum would get Dad on her side somehow, and the cause would be lost. There was nothing for it but to go round to this Schofield character's place once, collect the money for doing so and then cry off, pleading diminished responsibility. Fake nightmares might work – Emma did that all the time – or returning the money, nobly, with assurances that no financial reward could compensate for the terrible pity that

Mr Schofield's condition had wrung from his soul.

Mum and Emma were talking in the kitchen. Harry could picture the scene. He rolled over and looked at the plaster swirls on the ceiling. Mum would pour herself some stewed tea from the pot he had made, and sit down at the table with her shoes off. Emma would perch on the stool, kicking its legs, and soon she would begin to accuse him of taunting her, which was true, and hitting her, which wasn't.

He didn't understand what possible use he could be to Mr Schofield, whatever Mum said. It must be a wretched enough life without some dozy teenager turning up every five minutes, offering to play ludo with you. He frowned, wondering how a man who was able to move only his head could possibly get rid of an unwelcome visitor. Like someone in hospital, he couldn't get up and walk out. He just had to wait until the end of visiting hours, come what may.

It sounded like torture. Torture for Mr Schofield, and torture for Harry.

He stood up, took off his tie and undid the top button of his shirt. The lamps were just coming on in the street. He watched the headlights of a car swing around the corner, and the hall light snap on in the house opposite.

He'd have to endure the torture once, but once would probably be enough for both of them. Perhaps Mr Schofield would actually ask him, or even *pay* him, to leave.

The absurdity of this thought cheered him a little, and he turned from the window, wriggling out of his damp blazer. He'd change his clothes, and get warm, and perhaps things wouldn't look quite so hopeless. Dad hadn't named his price yet. Even on one visit, he might stand to make a reasonable profit. And Mum owed him forty pence for the "darlings".

"Harry!" Her calling-upstairs voice came out of the kitchen. "Come down here this minute and tell me what you did to Emma!"

WHITE ROOM

On Monday evening it rained. Not the drizzly rain of the past week, but a real *Singing in the Rain* downpour. Under his father's golf umbrella Harry waited, his legs trembling with cold and nerves, at Mr Schofield's front door.

The house was a nineteenth-century villa in the kind of terrace where people had laurel bushes for hedges and names like "Agincourt" on their gates.

He'd pressed the bell, and heard it ring inside the house, but nothing had happened.

Suddenly he was startled by a crackly voice. "Is that Henry Pritchard?"

He peered into the darkness of the porch. There was an intercom beside the door. "Yes," he said into it, feeling self-conscious.

"Push the door when you hear the buzzing noise, would you?"

There was no one in the hall, though the door to his right was open. Harry left his umbrella in the porch and stepped onto a black and white chessboard floor.

"Don't worry about leaving puddles." He was surprised by the strength and clarity of the voice. "Come in, then, and let's take a look at each other."

When he entered the room his first impression was of light. It was the brightest, cleanest room he had ever been in, with a ceiling as high as a church and walls unnaturally white, like the white clothes on detergent packets. At one end there was a huge window with white curtains open to the splashy darkness.

"Do I call you Henry, or something less important-sounding?"

Whirring softly towards him with surprising speed was an electric wheelchair, which arrested his attention, he remembered afterwards with shame, before he even looked at its occupant. It appeared to be operated by the man's chin pressing a pad, attached to a metal arm which came round from the back of the wheelchair. Harry stared. Then he noticed that the face above the chin pad was smiling, and waiting for an answer.

"Er ... people call me Harry."

"I'm Simon. Forgive me if I don't shake your hand, but you can shake mine if you like." His small round eyes blinked. Harry didn't move.

"Well ... maybe next time. Thank you for coming, Harry. Do you want to sit down, or explore?"

Harry looked round the room. In truth, he didn't want to do either. He wanted to go home. But the next two hours stretched out uncomfortably before him and he had to fill them with something.

"Explore, I think."

"Be my guest, then," said Simon. "Take off that wet coat and hang it behind the door – that's where your mother hangs her coat when she comes to see me. Wonderful woman, your mother."

Tell me about it, thought Harry, unzipping his coat. So wonderful that she persuades Dad to pay folding money for one of her patients to get overtime, regardless of the wishes of the part-time unqualified nurse.

"Ask any questions you want. Young people usually ask how I go to the toilet, but perhaps you're past that age. Though I'll still explain if you want me to."

Clearly, the white room was the centre of Simon Schofield's universe. Outside the enormous window, Harry suspected, would be the garden he was so fond of looking at. At the other end of the room was a high bed like a hospital bed, spread with covers as white as the walls. In one corner stood a television and video recorder, and in another a computer workstation. One of the walls was completely covered with shelves crammed with books, files and compact discs. And everywhere there were lights – on the ceiling, on tables, on tracks running round the walls.

"You see that I keep myself occupied," said Simon, as Harry's gaze fell on a very new-looking CD player and radio. "It's wonderful to have the gifts of sight and hearing." He looked up at him innocently. "That's irony, you know. I expect your English teacher has mentioned it."

The only question Harry could think of was so moronic he was too embarrassed to ask it. The room was full of things you couldn't work unless you could move your arms and hands. He stared at the computer. It was about twice as good as the one Dad had just paid a fortune for. But how did Simon use it?

"Are you always this quiet, Harry?"

His embarrassment increased. He opened his mouth, then closed it again.

"Want to see how it all works?"

Remembering the lecture Mum had given him about being polite to Mr Schofield, he found his voice. "Yes, please."

Simon nodded towards a black box about the size of a videotape case, attached to the arm of his chair. "Know anything about remote control?"

"A little." Very little, in fact. Fatso Collier was an awful teacher.

"Well, this console operates the things in this room by remote control, in exactly the same way as your handset operates the TV at home."

Harry frowned, only half understanding. "If the console controls the things, though, you must be controlling the console. Is that right?"

Simon nodded.

"But how do you do that?"

Every remote control handset Harry had ever seen had buttons on it, for people to work with their fingers. But the box on the wheelchair arm had no visible means of control at all.

"Watch this."

For the first time Harry saw a thin tube like a drinking straw positioned near Simon's mouth. It came out of another black box, which was attached to a flexible, angled support like the one on his desk-lamp at home, clamped to the back of the wheelchair. His bewilderment turned to interest.

Simon put his lips gently to the end of the tube and blew into it. He waited a few seconds while a light travelled down the console, then blew into the tube again. The TV leapt into life. Simon blew into the tube and the volume decreased. Then he blew again and the TV shut down. Harry was impressed.

"The console is modified to obey commands given by blowing into the tube," explained Simon. "It can operate all these gadgets, or change the lights, or open the front door, for instance. Still with me?"

Harry nodded.

"Of course," said Simon, "I've had to practise following the light and blowing at exactly the right moment. Closing the curtains when you mean to start the video recorder can be rather infuriating."

Harry sat down weakly on the arm of a chair. "It must be."

"When I was able-bodied, it never occurred to me any more than it has to you that the human lungs and windpipe can be as nimble as fingers. Possibly if I'd been a singer rather than an actor I might have known more about it. But this little tube *is* my fingers. Technology has brought me all this independence, and I'm very grateful to it."

He smiled encouragingly. "Come and sit in a comfier chair, and I'll see if I can blow into a tube which will activate Henry Pritchard."

Harry thought this was a weird thing to say, but he followed the wheelchair to the window and sat down in a large, sloppily-covered armchair. Simon parked facing the garden, looking out at the rain.

His face was mostly hidden behind a beard and long, though tidy, hair. But Harry could see that it had probably been handsome once. Despite the withering of the body beneath it, the thin hands and the turned-in feet, it gave an impression of style. And his clothes were carefully chosen too. Expensive, well-kept. His shoes shone and his hands and nails were far cleaner than Harry ever managed to get his own.

Washing them was a nurse's job, he supposed. And dressing him, and putting him into bed and getting him up, and brushing his teeth. Perhaps that's why he'd grown the beard, so that nurses didn't have to shave him too. And how *did* he go to the toilet? Harry had pictured a dribbling, helpless creature, but the real Simon was altogether more shocking.

He turned expectantly to Harry. "Now, what about telling me something about *you*?" It was the sort of thing teachers were always saying. But Simon didn't look as if he'd only be interested in

Harry's reply if the bell didn't go first. "Are you always so secretive?"

Harry didn't think he was being secretive. Boring, perhaps.

"Actually – " he began, then stopped. Why had his cheeks flushed? Surely the power of Louise wasn't strong enough to penetrate the white room?

"Go on," encouraged Simon.

He swallowed. "Did you say that when you were a young man – you were an actor?"

Simon's eyes closed and a satisfied smile spread over his face. He licked his lips contentedly and turned his head to one side. Opening his eyes, he gave Harry a sly look without turning his head back. Then he closed his eyes again, still smiling, and made a sound in his throat which sounded exactly like Razzle.

"Who am I?" he asked in his ordinary voice.

"You're a cat." The answer came to Harry almost at the same instant that he said it. Of course he was a cat. He was acting a cat, using only the muscles of his face.

"Just so. And you're a bright boy."

Harry was pleased. "What was it like, being an actor?"

Simon looked at him from between narrowed eyelids. "Your mother," he said slowly, "has not only sent me an intelligent boy, but one who possesses an interest in the theatre. Am I right?"

He flushed again. He couldn't rid his mind of the association between the word "theatre" and that unedifying encounter outside Miss Drew's room.

"I've never mentioned it to Mum," he confessed.

"That doesn't mean she doesn't *know*," said Simon. "Women have ways of picking up all sorts of information, I'm afraid. Usually the bits you'd rather they didn't."

"Unfortunately," said Harry, his flush diminishing.

"Yes, unfortunately!"

There was a silence while they both considered their common experience, and it occurred to Harry that this was what Mum had meant when she'd said that Simon could do with some male company. How could he complain, even jokingly, about women to women themselves? It would be like having to complain about Gerard Fox only to his slobbish, though less terrifying, older brother. He gulped silently at the thought.

Simon looked out at the darkness. His profile, white-lit by a fluorescent tube above the window, did look unnervingly like an actor's. "It was a wonderful profession," he said. "I was in it for ten years."

"What kind of things did you do?"

"Oh, Shakespeare – all the tragic roles. I liked Julius Caesar best. Lovely robes, lovely speeches. I had quite a few TV parts, too, and I enjoyed doing pantomime. My Puss in Boots is still talked about all over Accrington! Or was it Harrogate?"

Harry smiled at Simon's affectionate impression of a vain old actor. Simon smiled too. Then he looked serious again.

"I miss it, of course. But I won't have you thinking

that I haven't been grateful for the second half of my life as well as the first. Acting was important to me, but it isn't the only thing in the world. And anyway, as you've just seen, I can still do it whenever I want to."

Harry sat forward in his chair. "*How* do you do it, though?" he asked. "Without moving your body, I mean?"

Simon pressed the operating-pad with his chin and the wheelchair turned from the window. "Have you ever heard actors performing a play on the radio?"

"Yes, I think so." He was uncertain. "At school, perhaps."

"Well, how do you think they do it, when the audience can't even see them?"

"Oh, I see." His hair fell over his forehead. He pushed it back.

"Exactly. If you know the answer, why ask the question?"

Harry's school experience had taught him the wisdom of answering a question with another question. "But *you* did that, didn't you?"

"What?"

"Asked me a question when you already knew the answer. It's what teachers do all the time."

Simon's little eyes sparkled approvingly. "Very true! But I'm not a teacher, and I hope you'll forgive me for sounding like one."

"Oh – you didn't." He paused to work out what he was really trying to say. "I mean ... you showed me what I knew already without making me go through that performing-dog routine they always expect."

"And you don't want to be a performing dog?"

He felt as if Mr Mitchell had asked him to solve a problem aloud in front of everyone in his maths class. But Simon's scrutiny was far closer than theirs as he waited patiently for an answer Harry couldn't give.

"Well, I don't blame you one bit," he said at last. "I spent my entire schooldays hoping no one would notice me! Odd, when you consider the profession I ended up in."

"Yes," said Harry quietly.

He wondered what Simon's life had been like before, and what it was like now. He wondered how he had become an actor, and how things had gone so tragically wrong for him. Suddenly, questions fizzed up in his mind like the bubbles in a glass of Tonio's Coke-and-ice-cream. A pain like indigestion gripped his chest, but he selected the biggest question of all.

"What happened to you, Simon? How did you get like this?"

Neither the unexpectedness nor the audacity of the question seemed to surprise Simon. He turned the wheelchair again, and his gaze settled calmly on the garden.

"I went to a party, more than thirty years ago," he said. "I was a young man – single, thank goodness – in my late twenties. I went on my motorbike, and drank rather a lot of wine. I didn't see a car which didn't see me, and we had a right old smash-up. Then I woke up in hospital with doctors muttering about me to each other as if I were deaf or mental, and that was that."

He didn't look at Harry. He went on looking at the darkness. Harry suspected the story hadn't been aired for a while. He felt stirred, but embarrassed.

"I'm sorry," he began. "I mean, if you don't want to talk about—"

"No, no. Of course you must know."

He asked his next most important question. "And how did you get all this high-tech stuff? It must have cost an arm and a leg."

It was too late to pretend he hadn't said that. "I mean—"

"I know what you mean," said Simon kindly. "About ten years ago my Aunt Baba – yes, that really was her name – died and left me a large sum of money and this nice big house. So I was able to do up this room and achieve much more independence than I had before. I'm very, very lucky."

Harry stared at him.

"And don't say 'how can you say that?' Spend twenty minutes in the day room of a home for the severely disabled and you'll see why I'm lucky."

Harry understood. More questions reached the surface.

"Who looks after you? Gets your meals and so on?"

"Several people. Delightful ladies like your mother attend to all the boring physical stuff, and my housekeeper Mrs Driver cooks and cleans and does the laundry."

"How do you eat?"

"Mrs Driver feeds me. Her food is so delicious I can just about bear the indignity."

Harry was silent.

"No more questions? Trying to imagine what my life is like? Most people do that, but it's actually a waste of time. My life is in my head, just like yours."

There was a long pause. Harry wasn't sure if there *was* any life in his head. He felt as if he'd stumbled into an alien landscape without the means to survive.

"Do you like computers?"

Simon had turned the wheelchair away from the window, and was looking at him with interest. Harry tried to mould his features into an alert expression. "I'm not sure. I mean, the computers at school seem so ... well, *boring*."

"And so they are, when there's a room full of them, all staring at you like the front row of a first-night audience!" chuckled Simon. "One on its own is much more fun. A bit like girls, really."

Harry thought about the computer room at school. He'd never considered why he felt discomfited every time he entered it. But Simon was quite right. The rows of black screens *did* look hostile, and expectant, somehow.

"I couldn't do without mine now," said Simon, positioning the wheelchair at the workstation. "It relieves me of the dreaded mouth-writing, which I was never very good at. And, of course, it connects me with the rest of the world."

Harry blinked. "But how can you work it?"

"By using what actors use when they perform a radio play. Watch."

He blew into the tube, waited for the light on the console to reach COMPUTER, and blew again.

Wondering what was going to happen, Harry drew up a chair and sat down.

"Sleep no more!" cried Simon suddenly. Harry jumped involuntarily.

The computer screen presented several boxes, just like the one at home. Harry wondered how Simon would choose a box without using a mouse or a key. He tried to speak, but a tiny, warning shake of Simon's head silenced him. "Aroint thee, witch!"

He had evidently chosen the word-processor, which woke up and murmured busily. Harry saw the words NO SHADOWS appear on the screen. Simon contemplated them for a moment, absorbed in his own thoughts. "The rest is silence," he said, and the computer began to close down.

"It works by voice recognition," he explained. "I can write whatever I want, provided I don't go too fast."

"Just by *speaking*?" Harry was astonished.

"Just by speaking."

"It's really good," said Harry. Then something occurred to him. "But why didn't it write that stuff you said about not sleeping?"

Simon gurgled with laughter. "Sleep no more!

Macbeth does murder sleep!"

Harry looked blank.

"That line from *Macbeth* was my start-up command." He had stopped laughing, but his eyes shone like two gems in a jeweller's shop window. "You see, I've programmed this magic box to obey quotations from Shakespeare. Jolly, isn't it?"

Harry felt his jaw slacken. He tightened it as the amusement on Simon's face became kindness again. "The next time you come, Henry Pritchard, you won't even notice all this. I guarantee the extraordinary will quickly become ordinary."

But Harry wasn't supposed to be supplying a next time. He glanced at his watch. Then he stared at it. It said six minutes to eight. He shook it, and held it to his ear before noticing that Simon was laughing at him. "Dear me! Were you dreading me so much?"

Harry tried to keep the truth off his face.

"It's all right, dear boy. I can see you're itching to put yourself somewhere else. Go along, now. I'm a bit tired, anyway."

Harry jumped up. Then, noticing his rudeness, he collected his coat at a more casual pace, and zipped it up.

"Thank you for coming," said Simon good-naturedly. "Pull the front door hard behind you."

Harry's self-consciousness rose again. How could he walk freely out of the house, while Simon had to sit there, shackled to a wheelchair?

"It was really interesting. The computer and everything, I mean."

"Good. Thursday, then, at seven o'clock?"

"Er ... yes, all right." He opened the door.

"Good night, Harry."

"Good night."

It was still raining, but not so hard. Using the umbrella like a walking-stick, Harry walked quickly away, raindrops trickling down the back of his neck. At the corner of the street he stopped and looked back at Simon's house. It was absolutely, completely dark. The white room was at the back, spilling its light out onto the lawn.

He shuddered, and walked on. He refused to think about Simon sitting there alone, staring at the darkness. After all, the man himself had acknowledged that he was lucky, and grateful.

After all, Harry had problems of his own.

Tomorrow was his last chance this term to join the Drama Club. Miss Drew had put up a notice. Tomorrow, providing he could dodge Brig Fox as they came out of the dining room, he would make that trip to Miss Drew's room. And only after he'd done that would he allow himself to think about whether to go back, ever, to the white room.

He fitted his key into the front door lock.

"Is that you, Harry?" called Mum's voice.

Who else would it be?

"Going up for a shower!" he called, and made for the stairs.

Tomorrow or never, then.

SIMON SAYS

Lowth Heath, according to a booklet Harry had once flipped through in the public library, had been recognized for centuries as common land, where anyone could graze sheep or walk out with a young lady. Nowadays the sheep had given way to prowling dogs and couples wrestled on the grass rather than walked out. But despite the houses which surrounded the heath and the paths which criss-crossed it, it was still called the Heath and still looked a bit like one.

Harry hadn't been allowed to play there, and neither was Emma.

"Too many bushes," Mum declared. "Goodness knows who's hiding in them and what they're getting up to. You stay away from there."

"Too much dog poo," was Dad's contribution.

The houses in Lowth Heath had been built just after the Second World War. The estate agents in the High Street described them as semi-detached family villas. They had short front gardens and long back ones, with higgledy-piggledy sheds and greenhouses, and compost heaps that smelled in summer.

Harry went to school on the bus along the dual carriageway which led out of the city through Lowth Heath, with its building societies and shoe shops and the new American-style shopping mall. Every morning he passed Tonio's just as Tonio and Maggie were setting up the pavement tables.

Sometimes they waved, but Harry hardly ever waved back because it seemed such a nerdy thing to do in front of all the other Lowth Heath kids on the bus.

Friday night was Tonio's night. Harry would be there this Friday as usual, though he had to go and get his hair cut first. And Susannah Gold, who lived next door but one and had known him all his life, would be there too.

Stolz and Mig would come in at nine o'clock and order two Specials, which were pizzas as big as bicycle wheels which Harry could never get through. Then they would make two glasses of Coke last until half past ten.

Harry never knew what they did after that because he had to go home then, but Stolz and Mig were a year ahead of him at school and Stolz had a motorbike. They were all right. They never laughed because he had to catch the bus or ride his push bike. He hung around with them at school too sometimes, though Brig Fox's brother Roland was in their class, which was beginning to make things difficult.

The bus was early this morning. The tables and chairs were still piled up and the glass door with its sign announcing that Tonio's had hot and cold drinks, pizza, snacks and ice-cream and would be open at 8.45 was still bolted. As he got off the bus Harry planned that he would order a slice of plain pizza and an espresso, and maybe later have a Coke-and-ice-cream, with one of those paper parasols on the rim of the glass.

"Hey, Pritchard!"

That well-known sneering call, that kerb-scuffing, stone-dislodging shuffle.

Harry walked on with his head down.

"My brother says you're a queer."

A *queer*? What planet did these Foxes live on? No one had said queer for decades. It was a story to save for Stolz, though. Harry could hear the guffaw he'd make.

"Piss off, Fox," he said, "or I'll show you how queer I am, shall I?"

Fox crouched down and picked up a stone. They were still in the street, between the bus stop and the school gate. If Fox threw the stone there was little Harry could do. He didn't quicken his step, though.

It hit him squarely between the shoulder blades, like an Indian's arrow in a cowboy's back. He didn't turn round.

"Gerard Fox, stop right where you are!"

Mr Mitchell, guarding the gate as usual, picked up the stone. He aimed as if to throw it back at Fox, who ducked instinctively.

"Your brain's no bigger than this, is it?" he said, weighing the stone in his hand.

Harry didn't look at him as he passed. A teacher was a teacher, after all.

But Mr Mitchell caught his elbow with a grip like a mechanical claw. "I saw this, Pritchard. And it's not the first incident. If you haven't told your parents what Fox is doing, I will."

Harry couldn't think of many things more futile. It wasn't as if his dad was going to go round and beat up Fox's dad, or vice versa. His dad would give him a lecture about standing up for himself, and Fox didn't even have a dad.

"I'd rather you didn't mention it to them, sir," he said. "I can deal with Fox."

"Of course you can. Like you did just now, you mean?"

He couldn't stand the way Mr Mitchell thought he was a prat. "Please – just leave it a bit longer, will you, sir?" he pleaded.

Mr Mitchell let go of his elbow and fetched a long, quivering, mock-bewildered sigh. "Who exactly are you trying to impress, Pritchard? If it's me, you're failing."

Harry said nothing. His hair fell over his eyes.

"If you shrug I'll give you detention, boy."

He didn't shrug, but he still said nothing. Mr Mitchell pondered, then sighed again.

"All right. I don't know why I'm doing this, but you've got until the end of this term."

"Thanks, sir."

"Shake?"

Mr Mitchell's hand was large and dry, but unexpectedly soft. "Thanks again, sir," said Harry.

No sound came from inside Miss Drew's room, even after Harry's second, louder knock. He put his head furtively round the door. The room was empty.

The straight forelock of light brown hair – his only distinctive feature – fell into his eyes again. It was getting too long. He'd washed it and left it wet and combed it back this morning, like he always did. But by the time Mr Mitchell had stopped him at the school gate it had been flapping like a flag in the breezy sunshine, waiting for the first touch of his hand to turn it into greasy bootlaces.

He pushed it back and looked round the room carefully, as if Miss Drew might be hiding in a cupboard. Under his breath he muttered two or three swear-words. Below the window some younger boys were playing football, or the version of football demanded by the smallness of the space. He heard them calling to each other. The ball whacked against the wall.

His decision seemed to make itself. Miss Drew's desk was so untidy that there seemed little point in leaving a note, and still less in hanging around waiting for her. Sensing a feeling of release, halfway between relief and disappointment, he spun on the ball of his foot like a soldier and walked out of the room.

"Are you looking for me?"

By some quirk of the timetable, Miss Drew had

never taught him. But he knew her. Everyone at Beechwood knew her because she was always singing. Loudly in assembly and softly in corridors, or as she went in and out of rooms. He'd also heard a rumour that she'd trained to be a ballet dancer, and had only become a drama teacher by accident.

Looking at her as she walked towards him along the corridor, he believed the rumour. Her hair, which was escaping frizzily from a scarf designed to contain it, looked as if she dyed it blonde in the bathroom at home. Her arms were full of a pile of exercise books and a tape recorder. But the way her feet arched as they touched the floor gave her movements a special, weightless look.

"Drama Club?" she said as she reached the classroom door. "Oh joy, a male!"

Harry tried not to blush or mumble. "I hope I'm not too late."

"Not at all. In fact, you're just in time. Have you got a name?" She'd put on her spectacles and was rummaging in the chaos on her desk. "Better still, have you got a pen?"

He took his second-best cartridge pen out of his breast pocket. "My name's Henry Pritchard."

"Thanks." She unclipped the end of the pen. "Pritchard, did you say?"

"Yes."

"Form?" She was scribbling, and didn't look up.

"10N."

"Ah, Tenen!" She wrote it down. "What a relief to discover you really exist!"

Harry waited while she took a packet of strong-smelling egg sandwiches out of the drawer and bit into one. "Have you had lunch?"

"Yes, thank you." Lying to teachers again, Pritchard. But his stomach wasn't ready to receive Mum's Tuesday sandwiches. He thought for a moment. Cheese and tomato.

Miss Drew patted the chair beside her desk. As he sat down, her glance flicked down to his feet and up to the top of his head, then came to rest on his face. "How tall are you, Henry?"

"Six dead. I'm usually called Harry."

He looked at her, then at the floor, feeling trapped.

"Don't hide under all that hair," said Miss Drew. "If I can't see your face I can't communicate with you."

Teachers, he thought. Always thinking they can communicate with you.

"Sorry, miss," he said in the pitying tone which Mum could never tolerate. "It needs cutting."

Dad had asked him to get it done last weekend, telling him he looked like some damned half-witted carthorse. He didn't push it back.

Miss Drew sighed, and glanced again at her notes. "Acted before?"

"No. But—"

"Well, you're in luck. I've called the auditions for the play for one o'clock on Friday."

Harry's empty insides jumped. *Auditions?* What auditions? For what play? All he'd offered to do was join the Drama Club, possibly as the person who sweeps the stage or takes the tickets. Possibly.

Miss Drew smiled sweetly. "If you're not there the only excuse I'll accept will be your own or a close relative's sudden death."

He cleared his throat. "Miss Drew ... I'm not sure about acting in a play. I just thought—"

"Rubbish! We need *boys.* There are more girls in this school desperate to make public exhibitions of themselves than you've had hot dinners."

Or in the case of today, he thought, no dinner at all.

She tossed back her hair. It came forward again immediately. "Come on, Henry, why not give it a try?"

"I'm usually called Harry," he repeated.

Miss Drew smiled again. She had small teeth and bright pink lipstick. She reminded him of a doll Emma had abandoned years ago, which now lived at the bottom of a box in the garage. "I think I'll call you Tenen, since you're the only one of that species I'm ever likely to meet."

Harry said nothing. The desire to be somewhere else surged up and settled uncomfortably in his chest.

"Look." She handed him a book from a pile on the corner of her desk. Unwillingly, he took it. "This is the play we're doing at the end of term. Take it away and look at it, and let me know which part you'd like to read for."

"But honestly, miss..."

"And don't tell me you don't want to be in a play. Why else would you go to all this trouble to join us?"

She knows, thought Harry. She knows I'm only joining because I'm a dork.

He looked at the book. On its tatty paper cover he read the words "*Accelerando,* by E.E. Gibbard." He glanced back at Miss Drew, who raised her eyebrows. He drew a breath and let it out again.

A vision of burning boats filled his brain.

"I'll see you on Friday, in the hall. One dead, as you would say," said Miss Drew.

Resigned, he put the book in his bag. "It's not in Italian, is it, miss?"

"No, of course not." She looked at him sternly, though he couldn't tell how seriously. "I hope you're not a *joker,* Henry Pritchard. When you read the play you'll see the significance of the title."

"It's not a set text, is it?" he asked with sudden panic.

Miss Drew smiled widely, but didn't laugh. "No, it's not. I think you'll agree that when they start setting plays like this for examinations, examinations will be ... a bit different."

"I see," he said, though he didn't.

"Off you go, then." She went back to her sandwich, humming softly.

Dismissed, he walked to the door, then walked back. Miss Drew looked up.

"Save the questions until after you've read the play, Mr Tenen," she said pleasantly.

"I wasn't going to ask any questions," he said.

"At least, not about the play."

"What, then?"

"Er ... please could I have my pen back?"

Harry couldn't sleep. The darkness of the room and the tick-tocking of the alarm clock irritated rather than soothed him, until he was so restless that he got out of bed. If he used his brain, he reasoned, it might run out of energy, slow down and, eventually, stop.

The dog-eared corner of the playscript was sticking out of a pile of folders on his bedroom floor. He'd shoved it in there, hoping to forget it. But his thoughts kept returning to it, shunting along the same line as predictably as a train on a track.

First he would decide that the whole thing just wasn't on. What with visiting Simon, and doing his homework and everything, the idea of having time to devote to a play was perfectly ridiculous.

Then he would remember his motive for joining the Drama Club in the first place. Acting in a play with Louise would mean seeing her *a lot*. He imagined it. He imagined discussing with her how she should play a certain scene. He imagined how eager she would be to hear his opinions, and how informed and intelligent they would be.

Then he would imagine the audition.

Then he would go back to his original decision not to do it at all.

Then a picture of Louise's dark hair gleaming under the stage lights, her thin face brightened by make-up and nerves, would come into his head.

Within seconds he'd be back on the railway again, always heading for the next station but never reaching his destination.

He didn't know what destination he was trying to reach. He didn't even know whether he wanted to go back tomorrow night for another question-and-answer game in that strange colourless room. He knew still less what to do about the audition on Friday. The problem of Gerard Fox and his troupe of lackeys seemed comfortingly straightforward in comparison.

It was cold in the bedroom. Harry put on his dressing gown and sat on the floor in the light from the reading lamp. He touched the corner of the playscript tenderly, as if it might burn his fingers. Slowly, he removed it from the pile of folders and turned the first page. Where his dressing-gown crossed over his chest, his heartbeat moved the material up and down.

Get a *grip,* Pritchard.

"*Accelerando,* a Play in Two Acts by E.E. Gibbard", announced the frontispiece. A note at the bottom said that it had first been published fifteen years ago. He'd never heard of it. His parents only took him to children's shows suitable for Emma, and the plays he read about in newspaper reviews were always on in London, a place which seemed to Harry as remote from Lowth Heath as the Sahara Desert or the Great Barrier Reef.

There were four main characters, two men

and two women, and several others. TOADY, *a manservant* looked a likely one. He browsed on through the first few pages, screwing up his eyes. Then he took his spectacles from the bedside table drawer and put them on, and went on reading.

The play, he realized with surprise, was a comedy set in 1805 – a period of history completely outside his knowledge. It was full of lines like "In truth I know not, madam", and "Such wit cannot but delight me, I swear!", and had strange stage directions like *A trapeze swings slowly across the stage.*

Harry frowned, puzzled. He couldn't see much to laugh at. He dropped the book, took off his glasses and stood up. Stooping to the mirror which had been at the same height since he was ten years old, he sucked in his cheeks, making his thin face thinner. Louise had a thin face, he reflected, and she was always chosen to be in plays. Maybe you didn't have to look like an actor to be an actor.

He looked with loathing at the blotchy tea-leaf freckles on the bridge of his nose, and his narrow lips that turned down at the corners. He certainly didn't look like an actor, and he didn't even *want* to act in a play which had turned out to be such a disappointment. So where did he go from here?

Suddenly he knew where.

He would go back to Simon on Thursday, and ask what he should do. And whatever Simon said, Harry would have to do. Simon says, put your hands on your head. Simon says, scratch your nose.

That was the game, which he'd played so often with Emma when she was little.

Fatigue suddenly engulfed him. Yawning, he got back into bed and turned out the light. The play-script lay in a patch of moonlight on the bedroom floor. Harry looked at it calmly for a moment, then closed his eyes.

Now, he was certain, sleep would come.

FARCE

Harry pressed the buzzer, pushed the door, crossed the hall and went into the white room as if he'd been doing it all his life. He didn't even blink as the phalanx of lights assaulted his eyes.

"Hello again," he said.

Mum had seen Simon in the afternoon, and had reported to Harry that he seemed to be having a bad day. "He's a bit low, darling. See if you can cheer him up. Get him interested in something."

He left the playscript in the pocket of his coat and sat down beside Simon's chair. "Could you help me with something? I've got to make a decision by tomorrow, and I'd really appreciate your opinion."

Simon looked tired, but he answered in his usual voice. "Of course. Fire away."

He listened without interruption as Harry told him that he would quite like to be in the Drama Club without being in the play, but Miss Drew expected him to audition because he was a boy.

"If I'm going to make an idiot of myself," he confessed, "I'd rather do it in a good play. But this one's *awful.*" He frowned, and tried again. "I mean, it seems awful, from what I've read so far. But perhaps you can help me understand it better."

While Harry had been speaking Simon's tired look had changed. His blue eyes blinked rapidly. His eyebrows drew together in concentration. He thought for a few moments. Then he said, "Is there a young lady involved in this somewhere?"

There didn't seem much point in trying to pretend.

"Her name's Louise." He kept his voice as blank as he could. "Her other name's possibly Harding. She's one of Miss Drew's favourites, because she's really good at drama and music and speaking and so on. She's in my year, but not in my class, and Beechwood is such a huge school it's impossible to get to know anyone who isn't in your class unless you join a club, so I thought – well, you know the rest."

"And what is Miss Possibly-Harding like?" Simon asked seriously. "'She walks in beauty, like the night,' I trust?"

"Well..." He felt his face colouring, and stopped.

"That's my man. Obviously, you've got to do the audition whatever the damned play's like. Prop it up on my stand and let's look at it."

He knew the play already. "*Accelerando!*" he exclaimed. "But that's wonderful! I love that sort of stuff. All that pray-ing and nay-ing. Huge hit on the Edinburgh Fringe. God knows who E.E. Gibbard is – never heard of him doing anything since. But the play was very well received. I'm surprised you don't remember." He looked hard at Harry, then looked away again. "It's all right, Harry, I know you weren't born then. Let me have my little joke."

Harry thought he'd better ask an intelligent question. "What's the Edinburgh Fringe?"

Simon's eyes began to gleam. "Well, the Edinburgh Festival itself is an international arts festival held in Edinburgh every August. It's the biggest and most famous one in Britain. There's theatre and poetry and music and dance – everything, really. And in theory, anyone can perform anything at Edinburgh as long as there's a space for them to do it in. Those events are what people call the Fringe, because they're sort of outside the main events."

Mum would be proud of me, thought Harry.

"*Accelerando* is a riotous comedy," Simon went on. "It can bring the house down if it's done properly."

"Well, that's one of the things I want to ask you about. I can't see anything funny in it. And although it's supposed to be taking place ages ago it's got modern references in it. And the language is really weird."

Simon's eyes were scanning the first page. "Would you get that pencil? That's right, over there on the table."

Harry brought the pencil and held it out automatically. Simon raised his eyebrows. "*You're* doing the writing, Harry."

Feeling very foolish, Harry sat down heavily in the armchair.

"Now turn this page and let's get down to some work."

Work, thought Harry, turning the page. Work at school, work at home, work at Simon's. He wondered what he was missing on television. And what was he doing here anyway? Clutching at the one straw which might, at some unimaginable distant moment, rescue him from the top of Louise Harding's list of anoraks?

"The modern references are part of the comedy," Simon was saying. "And you have to admit they can be very funny. Haven't you seen *Blackadder*?"

Harry was unconvinced, but he began to listen as Simon read the first scene aloud. His voice was clear and calm, and he didn't try to show off by producing a different voice for each character. He didn't sound besotted with his own talent, either, like the people who read novels aloud on the tapes Mum listened to in the car.

For the first time Harry began to understand what the play was about.

It was a pretty stupid story, about stupid men getting their girlfriends mixed up. But he could see what Miss Drew meant about it being unsuitable for examinations. Some of it was surprisingly rude.

"So which character are you going to audition for?"

Simon was looking at him with an intent, questioning look. Harry looked back more vaguely.

"Er ... Toady? He's only a manservant, and doesn't say anything."

"Leave him to a toad, then," said Simon emphatically. "Read for a part that demands the use of your wits, since you've got some."

Harry was flattered. "Which one do you suggest, then?"

Simon nodded towards the scene which lay open on the stand. "What about Malcontent?"

Malcontent appeared in the cast list as MALCONTENT, *a villain*. In the scene they had just read he had tried, with some sexy talk, to persuade a maidservant to spy on her mistress for him.

"I can't do that. It's got too much talking." And it's embarrassing, he might have added.

"No it hasn't. Malcontent's only in about half a dozen scenes." Simon's face took on a crafty expression, and his eyes began to glow. "But he's absolutely crucial."

Harry took the script off the stand and flipped the pages. It was true that Malcontent said far less than the four main characters involved in the mix-up. Sometimes he was in a long scene without saying anything except to the audience. And the speeches he did have often consisted of two rhyming lines, which looked easy to learn.

"At the very beginning Malcontent goes out there on his own," said Simon. "His job is to set the scene and catch the audience's interest. And his name's significant, you know. A malcontent is a man who feels hard done by, and wants revenge on those he feels have wronged him. The audience know what he's really doing, but he manipulates the other characters into believing he's their friend. I think it's a wonderful part, and I wish I'd played it."

"You're just saying that, Simon."

"Rubbish! Do you think I'd flatter you? I'd love to have the chance to snarl at the audience, and behave in a totally disgusting and repellent way."

Harry's heart rate quickened. The audience for the play would consist of parents, teachers and school governors. "Really?"

"Yes, *really*." He sounded impatient. "Come on, let's try and get through the first act tonight."

It took a long time, because Simon kept dictating things for Harry to write in the margin. By half past eight Harry was exhausted.

"Mrs Driver's left some chocolate cake for you in the kitchen," said Simon as Harry closed the book. "You know how to make instant coffee, don't you?"

When he came back with the tray Simon had gone over to the window. His eyes looked thoughtful, as if he were trying to imagine something he'd long forgotten. "Low-necked dresses, and cheeky little bonnets," he murmured. "It was a man's world in those days, right enough!" He broke into a chuckle. "I wish I were you, Harry!"

Not because I can walk and use my arms, he thought. Affected by Simon's unselfish envy, he looked hard at the tray as he put it down.

"I wish you were me, too. I wish you could do the audition for me."

"Are you going to do it, then?" asked Simon, his eyes brightening.

Harry played the game. "Do you think I should?"

"Dear boy, I insist!"

"Simon says?"

"Simon says."

Simon's voice was full of relief and satisfaction. "But," he added, looking at Harry from under lowered eyelids, "if the lovely Louise turns out to be a sack of potatoes, I don't give refunds. You're on your own."

"This isn't one dead!" cried Miss Drew, stopping outside the main door. She was smiling her rosebud smile. "It's six minutes past. You're late."

"So are you," said Harry before he could stop himself.

She looked amused. "I'm always late. But that doesn't mean you can be. Come on, let's go in together."

He was resigned to his fate. But when they reached the hall, resignation turned to fear, and then panic. Miss Drew grabbed his blazer sleeve with fingers of steel and pulled him smartly between the swing doors.

"Here we all are, then!" she trilled, without letting go.

The first two rows of chairs were full of people, nearly all of whom he didn't know. Without exception, they stared at him.

Miss Drew took a sheaf of papers from her briefcase and handed it to him.

"You can hand these out, Mr T."

Trembling, he did so. The pieces of paper were photocopies of two or three different scenes from the play. Simon had insisted that Harry read Malcontent's opening lines on Thursday evening, between mouthfuls of the best home-made chocolate cake he'd ever eaten. "I won't get chosen," Harry had assured him as they'd parted. But Simon had just smiled.

In the front row were three dark-haired girls. The first one wasn't Louise Harding, but the second one was. She took the paper without looking at him, and moved her legs, which were crossed at the knee under her smooth grey skirt, out of his way. She was wearing black tights and polished black shoes.

He gave the spare papers back to Miss Drew and sat down. Louise Harding was out of sight. He shifted his chair slightly.

"As you've realized by now, the play is *Accelerando* by E.E. Gibbard, a period comedy which gives everyone the chance to wear silly hats and act the fool," announced Miss Drew. A groan went round. "Shut *up*. It's a good school play because it's got easy sets and enough characters, and it's funny and a bit rude, but not too unsuitable for parents. Any questions?"

Louise had the slimmest, straightest shoulders he'd ever seen. As she put up her hand he saw her right shoulder blade move under her blouse.

"Please, Miss Drew, why is it called

Accelerando?" she asked. "I mean – isn't that something in music?"

A few people tittered. Show-off, thought Harry.

Miss Drew spread her hands on the lid of the grand piano. They were so thin they looked like a bird's claws. She had no spare flesh anywhere on her body. He wondered whether he, skinny though he was, would be able to pick her up and put her on his shoulder, like he'd seen male dancers do on television. He tried to imagine what it might feel like.

"Louise is perfectly right. The term *accelerando* is a musical one, meaning to get faster. Those of you who haven't read the play, or perhaps even those of you who have" – she shot him a glance which lasted no more than a nanosecond – "may like to know that the play is organized like a dance, which starts off slow and gets faster. It's as simple as that."

It didn't sound simple at all. Simon hadn't said anything about *dancing*. Harry swallowed uncomfortably.

"Is it a musical, then, miss?" asked the red-haired girl sitting next to Louise.

"No, it's a farce."

"A what?" exclaimed the girl, amid howls of laughter. "Sounds like something else, miss!"

Harry found himself smiling. The atmosphere around him had suddenly relaxed, and he realized for the first time that he was not the only one feeling nervous. The girl with her stupid comment had pole-axed the tension.

"All right, Patsy. Very funny. A farce is a special kind of comedy which involves careful timing, like a dance. Opening a door a moment too early or arriving on stage a moment too late can spoil everything. You'll soon see how it works when we start rehearsals. Thank you for the question, Louise."

Louise smiled without showing her teeth. Her pale, contoured face always looked intelligent to Harry, though he had yet to find proof of any intelligence behind its alert expression. And her voice, which he had often heard in assembly because she was always being chosen to read things, was extra clear without being extra loud.

Miss Drew organized groups of people to read the scenes. "Did you decide which character you want to read, Harry?" she asked.

His voice fell into silence like a stone into a pool. "Malcontent, I think."

"Good. We want someone tall and impressive-looking for the baddie, don't we? Come over here and stand by Patsy O'Donnell."

By some stroke of heavenly providence, Louise wasn't in his group.

She auditioned for BELLADONNA, *a poisonous beauty*, doing it so well that it was obvious that Miss Drew would choose her. She knew it, too, and received her friends' applause like a professional. Harry chewed his lip.

In his group, all the boys were awful. One of them could barely even read, and was soon tactfully directed towards backstage work by Miss Drew. As Malcontent's lines approached, he began to sweat.

Everyone was listening. Louise and everyone else. When he started to read, she would hear him. Inside, silently, she would laugh. He could hear her silent laughter as he stared at the words.

MALCONTENT, said the capital letters. The moment had come.

Suddenly, he thought of Simon. He saw him in his chair, purring, washing his nose with paws that weren't there. Of course, of *course.* How could he have been so thick? He wasn't just required to *read* Malcontent, he was required to *act* him, like Simon had acted the cat.

What was Malcontent like? He feels hard done by, Simon had told him. He's determined to take revenge. So what could he do? What would Simon do in this situation?

He pushed back his hair and narrowed his eyes. He produced a voice pitched lower than his own, and read the words more slowly than he would normally speak. He waited while someone else read their part, and narrowed his eyes again. Because Malcontent was supposed to fancy ANGELICA, *a sweet lady*, whose lines were being read by the auburn-haired girl, he had to be nervous with her.

Acting that was easy. He crossed and uncrossed his legs, and blinked fast as he said the words. By keeping his eyes on the page, he almost managed to forget that everyone in the room was staring at him.

At the end, he felt hot and sick, as if he'd been within centimetres of a fatal car crash. Miss Drew, her eyes shining behind her glasses, came up and poked him in the chest. "Malcontent!" she declared to the room at large.

No one said anything.

"You're the one who gets to swing on the trapeze!" said Miss Drew in a singsong voice.

Oh my God, thought Harry. That must be in the second act, which he and Simon hadn't got round to reading.

Everyone was catcalling and giggling. Even Miss Drew was laughing.

"Are your muscles up to it, do you think?" she asked Harry.

Patsy reached across and squeezed his upper arm. "Well, *I* think they are!" she announced to even louder squalls of laughter.

He knew that if he died then, in the school hall in the middle of a Friday lunchtime, he wouldn't mind. His face had never felt so hot. His inadequacies had never felt so exposed. At least when he'd led the sprint race on Sports Day in his last year at primary school, and had fallen over fifteen centimetres from the tape, he'd been able to run away. He had run across the field and hidden behind the lemonade tent until his parents came to take him home.

But today there was nowhere to hide.

That's why Miss Drew had given him the part, then. No one else wanted to be Malcontent. Everyone else knew you had to swing on a trapeze in front of hundreds of people, but he was too pathetic to have discovered this.

As his flush faded he stole a glance at Louise's back. He watched her hand gather the curtain of glossy hair into a ponytail, twist it round a few times, then let it go, so that it spun once again into freedom, settling on her shoulders like a hood.

Thinking about acting in the play with her restricted his breathing. He stared hard at the school crest on its shield above the stage. The two lions faced each other, each with a paw in the air, just as they always did. She might look terrible in the costume, anyway. She might have scrawny arms, with freckles on them worse than the ones on his nose, or...

"Is your name Henry Pritchard?"

She had sat down on the empty chair beside him, her playscript in one hand, the other resting in her lap. The smell of clean hair and some sort of sugary, cosmeticky scent reached his nostrils.

"Yes." The word struggled out though he had no breath to say it.

"Well ... hello." She seemed embarrassed. "I'm Membership Secretary of the Drama Club. It's nice to see someone new joining, and being in the play, but I'm afraid I need one pound fifty from you."

Harry wished he could laugh. But at this moment he knew that even a smile would crack his face, causing extreme pain.

"I haven't got any money on me," he said. Then

he added truthfully, "except my bus fare."

"Can you bring it on Monday? The first read-through of the play is on Monday after school. Bring it then and I'll give you your membership card."

"All right. Thanks."

"Right then."

She seemed to have completed her errand, but made no move. She gazed for a while at the school crest, just as Harry had done, then she turned back. He'd never seen her face so closely before. She wasn't looking directly at him, but had lowered her glance to somewhere around the knot of his tie, so that her eyelashes obscured her expression. "My name's Louise Harding," she said. "I'm in 10V."

"I know," said Harry.

This was only a statement of fact, and he was unprepared for its effect.

She lowered her chin and raised her eyes. The faintest glow of pink started up at the bottom of her cheeks. Harry was astonished.

"Everyone knows you because you're always in things," he added.

She looked at him squarely. Her eyes, he noticed, were grey and green all mixed up. One of them was slightly greener than the other. "Oh," she said, sliding the grey-green circles sideways before her head caught up with them.

It was a move he'd seen actresses make in films. She must have practised it in front of a mirror. "Well, I suppose that's true."

She really was stuck up. He couldn't excuse her,

though in truth he had no need to. She would never be interested in him except as a source of one pound fifty.

She stood up. “I’ll see you on Monday, then.”

“Yep.”

“’Bye.”

“’Bye.”

When she returned to her seat Harry could see her whispering with Patsy O’Donnell, who flicked a glance in his direction. He looked away, feeling an idiot. Patsy was the sort of girl who specialized in making boys feel idiots. The arm-squeeze she’d given him was typical of those girls. He could bet that she kicked boys’ ankles accidentally-on-purpose under the tables in the dining room. At Monday’s rehearsal she would probably admire his new haircut, and insist on touching it.

But girls like Louise, bright-looking but cool, who never put themselves in his way and never made excuses to touch him, were always the ones that he wished would do so. Where was the justice in that?

TONIO'S

Susannah Gold had always been unlucky for Harry. When they'd played together as toddlers she seemed to have no conception of danger, and having survived escapades which still made him go cold to think of them, she would screech at him until he tried them too.

At primary school it had been the same. He'd made up a rhyme about her and chanted it in the playground. "Susannah Gold, brave and bold, I hope she'll die before she gets old." This had led, predictably, to one of Dad's Talks.

"Explain yourself, Harry," he'd coaxed him. Harry must have been about eight. "Why would you say such mean things about Susannah?"

"What about all the mean things she says about me?"

"Nonsense. She's a lovely little girl."

"She is *not*."

"Now, Harry..."

"She's horrible and I hate her."

"Do you want to feel the back of my hand?"

Dad had never struck him, or Emma. Harry had known even then that he never would. Suggesting it was just his way of losing his temper. Harry used to wonder why anyone would hit someone with the *back* of their hand anyway.

When he'd gone to Beechwood Comprehensive, Susannah's parents had sent her to a girls' school where they had to pay fees. The uniform, which Mum said was the colour of the stuff in babies' nappies before they started to eat solid food, made golden-haired Susannah look hideous. Harry had joined in the general derision when she got on the bus that first day, but he had been the only boy punished for her tears. And because she lived so close and their mothers were friends, he couldn't get rid of her. She just went on turning up like a losing lottery number, getting taller and thinner but not much less annoying.

"Harry! Fancy seeing you here!"

Harry had an appointment with Ramon, who waved his scissors when he saw him come in. Ramon's partner, Yvette, was blow-drying Susannah's hair into a sleek, polished halo.

"Hello, Susannah," said Harry. Yvette, who sometimes cut his hair, smiled conspiratorially over Susannah's head.

"I'm almost finished," said Susannah, grinning at his reflection. "I'll wait for you and we'll go on to Tonio's together, shall we? Do you like my hair?"

He didn't answer. Don't rabbit on, Susannah, just

don't. As he thrust his arms into a stained nylon gown, she gave him one of her kittenish looks.

"I've been keeping this chair warm for you!"

After a small struggle with the nylon gown he found his left wrist. His watch said five past seven, and his spirits dived. Susannah's company would be exclusively his for at least an hour.

Girls, he thought exasperatedly as he sat down. How many must there be in the world? How many even in Lowth Heath? But which one was he going to walk into Tonio's with tonight? Susannah stop-me-talking-if-you-can Gold.

When they opened the door Tonio's was almost empty. The pretend-marble tables and the little bentwood chairs were all in their proper places, and the menu cards were still propped up with the salt and pepper pots as bookends.

Maggie, Tonio's wife, was putting a cup of coffee and a slice of apple pie down on the only occupied table. She nodded to Harry and Susannah.

"You early tonight, aren' you? Goin' to pictures?"

Harry liked the way she talked. It sounded as if the beginnings and endings of the words had been hacked off with a blunt instrument. He and Susannah climbed on to the old-fashioned chrome and leather bar stools. "We were both getting our hair cut at Ramon's," he said, "so we came straight here afterwards."

Maggie smiled broadly. "I see."

"It was just a *coincidence,* Maggie," he protested

mildly.

She giggled, looking at his, then Susannah's, hair. "Ver' nice. What you have?"

He ordered his pizza slice and espresso as planned. Susannah wanted black coffee. He had never seen her eat anything in public.

"You don't eat much, do you?" he said, realizing he'd known this for ages but had never taken any notice of it.

"Oh, Harry, of course I do!" She watched herself in the mirror behind the bar, smoothing her hair, which was already immaculately smooth. "But I try to eat healthily. And I don't like pizza."

Harry tried to imagine not liking pizza. When his slice arrived it looked and smelled even better than he'd anticipated, with the crust crispy and the cheese bubbling and the sauce escaping from underneath it as if it couldn't wait to get to his mouth.

As he ate, Susannah talked, and he let her. But three bites before the end of the slice she said something which stopped him swallowing. He put the pizza crust back on the plate and licked his fingers, watching her face.

"So I said to her, I said, you're sad, Patsy O'Donnell. And your hair looks like those horrible sun-dried tomatoes you buy in a jar. She's got this red hair, Harry—"

"How do you know Patsy O'Donnell?"

"Well, I just *told* you." She paused, eyeing him suspiciously. "You weren't listening, were you? She used to be in my Guide pack. So how do *you* know her, then?"

"She goes to my school. I think she's OK, actually."

He had said this to unsettle her, and it did. She stared at him, her prettiness blotched with dismay. "Harry, she's *awful.* Let me tell you what happened next."

He had no desire to hear, but his senses had been alerted. It was like a pattern. It was like the last piece of a jigsaw puzzle, fitting in.

"She was so mad her face went practically purple. But I soon put her in her place. I've got a much stronger personality than her, I think. And as for that toffee-nosed friend of hers ... well!"

Harry's heart leapt. The pizza had turned into tomato-flavoured cardboard in his mouth. "What friend?"

"This girl, Patsy's friend. She was *horrible* to me. She called me stick insect, which I thought was pretty immature. You've got to be thin to be a model, haven't you? She's just jealous of me because I've got blonde hair and hers is so dark. I don't like dark hair, do you, Harry?"

He was used to the banality of Susannah's prattle, but this opinion was far-fetched even by her standards. Especially since Tonio was standing no more than a metre away, cleaning glasses. Both he and Maggie, who wasn't actually Italian but Romanian, had beautiful dark hair.

"What's her name, this girl?"

"I *told* you, cloth-ears! What's the matter with you tonight? You're not concentrating." Her voice was getting squeaky. "Her name's Patsy. Pat-sy!"

Patience, Pritchard. "No, the other one. The one you don't like. With the dark hair."

"I don't know," she said sulkily. "Lisa? Lindsay? Something like that."

"Laura?" he suggested. "Louise?"

"Oh yes, Louise! How clever of you!"

"I know her, too. I'm in a play with her and Patsy at school."

It was the first time he'd announced this aloud. He felt as if he'd been thrust out on to a balcony to address a hysterical crowd. But Susannah wasn't looking at him, and didn't notice his blush.

"Are you really?" She admired her reflection, tinging her teaspoon against her saucer. "*I'd* like to be in a play. I think I'd be drop-dead good at acting. We used to play at dressing-up when we were tiny, didn't we? I was Cinderella and you were Prince Charming. We must have been so sweet!"

Harry didn't trust himself to be polite.

"This Louise – she used to go to my riding school." Susannah picked up her cup but put it back without drinking anything. "I still go, of course, but she was *useless*." She gave him one of her cover-girl looks, fanning her eyelashes out along her browbone. "Oh, Harry, I hope she's better at acting than riding!"

"Thanks, Susannah."

After this moment of concern, her unsinkable selfishness bobbed back to the surface. "It was really unfair, you know," she said crossly. "Her parents promised to buy her a pony, but mine say they can't afford it even though I'm really good at riding. Don't you think life's unfair sometimes?"

Throughout this speech Harry had been physically conscious of his heart sinking. He picked up his own coffee cup. "Her parents have got money, then?"

"Oh, loads! She lives in Chesterhill, in one of those big houses overlooking the golf course. My mother says she can't understand why Louise doesn't go to St Ursula's. They must be communists or something."

Harry would normally be amused at this sort of Susannah-nonsense. But tonight he couldn't dredge up a smile. Stuck up, show-off *and* posh. It was too much. And he was probably right about the ponies on the bedroom wallpaper. Being intelligent and talented – even being terrible at riding – couldn't cancel out such glaring inadequacies.

"I'll come to see the play and applaud the loudest, even if those horrible girls are in it," Susannah reassured him, with a smile as bright as a lighthouse beam.

As she raised her coffee cup to her lips he acknowledged that given the choice between her glowing face and Louise's pale one, some people might consider that Susannah was the girl they'd rather walk into a room with.

"Thanks, Suke," he said.

"Don't call me that."

"Why not? It's a term of endearment. You can

call me darling if you like."

"Oh, shut *up*, Harry."

At least she could tell he was teasing her. But she'd gone very, very red.

A noise at the door made them both turn round. Stolz and Mig trooped in like a line of recruits, wearing leather jackets and carrying crash helmets.

"Hey," they said to Harry and Susannah, which was what they always said.

"Hey," said Harry and Susannah.

"You're early," added Susannah.

Stolz put his helmet on the floor and sat down on one of the little chairs, which looked as if it would collapse under him. Stolz wasn't exactly fat, but large.

"We were at Mig's but his folks are having a party tonight," he explained. "His mum threw us out."

"You're looking gorgeous tonight, Suke," said Mig to Susannah. His real name was Martin but even teachers didn't use it much.

"Don't call me that."

Maggie came up with her notepad and pencil. "Don' you thin' Susannah's hair look good tonight?" she said. "She been in hairdresser with Harry."

Stolz and Mig exchanged looks. "Ooh!" said Stolz, rolling his eyes.

"Just because you fancy her—" began Harry.

"Shut it, Pritchard," said Stolz.

"You wan' make order now?"

Harry watched Maggie's round, fleshy face concentrating as she wrote. He wondered what she thought of Stolz, Mig, Susannah and himself. She saw them every Friday, and she was always polite and cheerful because her livelihood depended on people coming back to the café and bringing their friends. But did she know that Stolz, though built like an articulated lorry, was kind-hearted and nursed a passion for Susannah? Had she noticed that Mig, who as far as Harry knew had never had a girlfriend, liked to style himself as a lecherous dandy, with his comb never out of his hand? And did she ever wonder why Susannah was lonely enough to chase the boy-next-door-but-one?

"Hey, Harry!" Stolz turned round precariously on his chair. "There's a speedway meeting on Monday. You coming?"

Harry had been to the speedway stadium with Stolz before, and enjoyed it. The smell of hot tyres and the distorted buzz of pop music bouncing off the roof had stayed in his memory a long time. "Great," he said.

"I'll pick you up on the bike about seven fifteen."

He was halfway through agreeing to this when three separate objections fell into his head all at once. "Stolz – I can't, on Monday. I've got to do something else."

Three pairs of eyes looked at him expectantly. "Like what?" said Mig.

"I've got a rehearsal for the play."

"What play?" asked Stolz. He said it as if being in a play was only one level up from stepping in something disgusting on the pavement.

"A play he's in at school," supplied Susannah.

"At *school*?" The words were a sneer. "How long's it going to take, for God's sake?"

"I don't know." Harry wondered why he was having to defend himself. It was only speedway, after all. It was only a play. "It's the first rehearsal. But anyway, I've got to go out somewhere else afterwards."

They all stared at him doubtfully.

"I have, honestly."

Stolz turned back and muttered to Mig that if Harry didn't want to come to speedway all he had to do was say so.

"I *do* want to come," protested Harry, "but I can't. I've got a prior engagement."

"He's got a *job,* Stolz," said Susannah unexpectedly. "He goes on Monday and Thursday nights. Don't you, Harry?"

Harry clenched his fists under the counter. He felt like a kettle whose switch-off mechanism is broken, and just goes on boiling for ever and ever. How *could* Mum have told Susannah's mum about Simon, so that Susannah's mum could tell Susannah?

"What's this job, then?" asked Stolz.

Tonio brought the pizzas at that moment and Harry had time to think.

"It's just visiting someone," he announced casually. "An old man who doesn't get out much, and needs help with things. My dad pays me to do it."

"How much d'you get?" asked Mig, busy with his pizza.

"Enough."

"That much!"

"What's it to you?"

They munched without talking for a while, then Stolz's ponderous thought-processes went back to the subject. "Can't you go another night? What's wrong with Tuesday?"

"Not at short notice like this," said Harry, surprised at how easy it was to make things up as he went along. "I mean, he'll be looking forward to seeing me on Monday. He's a bit senile."

"Well, he won't know if it's Monday or Tuesday then, will he?"

Harry sighed. Stolz always showed intelligence when you least expected it. "Not *that* senile."

"Phone him up and tell him you've got something else to do on Monday," suggested Mig.

"I can't phone him up."

They were all suspicious, even Susannah. "Isn't he on the phone?" she asked.

The tension in Harry's chest subsided a little. She was either tactfully offering him help, which was unlikely, or she didn't know much about Simon after all. "No, he's not. I'll have to go on Monday. I've got no choice."

They seemed unconvinced. Harry ate his second slice of pizza distractedly, trying to establish why he had no choice. It was clear he couldn't let Simon down, but why?

Mig pushed his chair back. "Well, I don't believe a word of it," he said, looking slyly at Stolz. "I think he's got a hot date. What's her name, Pritchard?"

"Simone," said Harry, relieved that the conversation had touched down again on normal ground. Mig could be relied upon to reduce everything to his special level of tackiness. And neither he nor Stolz, nor Susannah, nor anyone he could think of at school, would ever understand about Simon.

Susannah rested her elbows on the bar and put her chin in her hands. She kept her back to the boys, but looked at their reflections in the mirror.

"Well, I think it's really nice of Harry to do such a worthwhile thing, instead of watching a bunch of amateurs skidding round a smelly old motorbike track. I wouldn't go speedway racing with you even if you asked me, Christopher Stolz."

Stolz looked at his feet.

"But I might go to the cinema."

During the laughter and embarrassed protests which followed this, Harry thought about his third reason for not going out with Stolz on Monday night.

He'd never considered it before, when Mig had given up first claim on the pillion seat and Harry had been whizzed home, frozen to the bone. But what if a car should pull out and fail to see them? What if Stolz, who often turned round to speak to him while they were on the bike, didn't see the car?

Being scared to get on a motorbike out-dorked all his other dorkishness. But it was a thought. It was definitely, terrifyingly, a thought.

MONKEY

Harry's visits to Simon sometimes lasted much more than two hours, but he couldn't ask Dad for overtime money because it was usually Harry himself who didn't notice how late it was. And rehearsing the play took up much more time than he'd anticipated. By the time two weeks had passed he'd started having to do his homework on the bus, and on the Monday of the third week of rehearsals Mum had to call him six times before he noticed it was morning.

That evening he laughed until his stomach ached at Simon's account of how his false moustache fell off during the most serious scene in *King Lear*, and lay on the stage like a small, furry, dead animal until another actor managed to kick it into the orchestra pit. Harry was about to accuse him of making up every word of it, when sudden pity, so crushing that he could offer it no resistance, drenched him like a power-shower.

He stopped laughing. He watched Simon's hollow,

once-muscular face, and the wasted limbs, whose movements had commanded the attention of so many audiences, and deep inside his head a shadowy, furtive thought formed.

"Can I ask you something, Simon?"

"Fire away."

Harry loaded his question, and fired.

"When you first had your accident, did you – I mean, did you..."

But his courage had scattered, and he couldn't find the pieces.

"Want to kill myself?" suggested Simon.

"Well, yes."

What a gross thing to say. Pink-cheeked, he waited for Simon to join the chorus of people telling him what a cretinous fool he was.

But Simon seemed lost in thought. The light from a spot lamp shone on his nose and brow. It was so quiet in the room Harry could hear his own breathing. At last, in a soft, measured tone, Simon spoke.

"Have you ever seen a play, or a film, called *Whose Life Is It Anyway?*"

"No."

"Well, in the story a man who was a brilliant sculptor has a car crash and is crippled just like I was. Can't move anything except his head. Hard, hard work for an able-bodied actor, because of course they wouldn't dream of casting a *real* quadriplegic actor."

Harry began to feel better. He hadn't offended

Simon after all.

"Now, the playwright had to make him a sculptor so that he could argue that if he couldn't use his hands there was no point in his life, and he should be allowed to die. For the whole length of the play the sculptor and the doctors argue and argue, and in the end they let him die. Well, that was a nice dramatic ending, but it made me very angry."

He paused, breathing quickly, and took a few sips of water from the bottle clamped to the arm of the wheelchair.

"Why?" asked Harry.

"Because I knew from experience that not being able to do what you did before is no reason to give up living. As long as you've got your head, you've got your life. Of course, severe brain damage is another matter, and if I get started on that we'll be here all night."

Harry thought he understood. "But did you actually consider – you know, killing yourself? When the accident first happened, I mean?"

"Of course. Everyone does." Simon's eyes gleamed. "But how do you kill yourself, if you can't move? Even death by computer needs an accomplice."

Harry's insides felt empty suddenly, as if he hadn't eaten for days.

"When you come on Thursday," said Simon briskly, "we'll look at my press-cuttings. That'll show you what I mean when I say I'm grateful for both halves of my life."

"You mean," said Harry with a flash of

inspiration, "that the person you are now can still be the person you were then, when you look at the cuttings?"

"Exactly. Now let's shut up about this and concentrate on things that really matter. Has Malcontent got up on the trapeze yet?"

As he left the locker room after rehearsal a couple of days later, Harry saw Louise Harding about two metres ahead of him. It was a bitter, frosty night. She was hunched up in her navy blue school duffle coat with a scarf wound round her neck and mittens on. Harry had left the house that morning without his gloves, regretting it by the time the bus came. And now, because the rehearsal had finished so late, he would have to wait for the bus in the dark *and* cold.

He caught her up before he could change his mind and walked beside her, trying to make sure his long legs didn't go too fast for her, which his mother always complained about.

"That was our worst effort ever, wasn't it?" he said.

"What?" She didn't look at him.

"The rehearsal. And I don't see how she can expect us to learn our lines by *Monday*. I mean, today's Wednesday, isn't it?"

She didn't reply. She was walking with her head down. In a moment of panic, he wondered if she were crying. "Are you all right?"

Her head came up, and he saw that although her face was composed, some sort of agitation had brightened her eyes. "Yes, thank you," she said politely.

He pressed on. "Why have we got to learn it so soon? We don't perform it until the last week of term, which is five weeks away."

"I wouldn't complain. I bet you could learn your part in one evening."

She looked at him then, and because she had to turn her head he knew she was looking at him. "Listen," she said. "If Miss Drew says books-down on Monday, she means it. You can't do a fast-moving play like this with books in your hands. You just have to get on and learn it."

Harry felt a bit put down. "Are you walking to the bus stop?"

"No. My mother's waiting, with the car."

A spasm of embarrassment passed through him. He knew what she was going to say, and she said it.

"We could give you a lift, if you like. Where do you live?"

His heart bulged against his side like a football in the goal net. "Lowth Heath." He watched her reposition her bag on her shoulder. It looked very heavy, but he couldn't be so uncool as to offer to carry it for her.

"I always think you have to say 'Lowth Heath' as if you've got a lisp," she said shyly, beginning a smile. "I know a girl called Susannah who lives there."

They'd almost reached the gate, but Harry steeled his nerve.

"Susannah Gold, do you mean?" he asked.

"Yes!" Her breath made a cloud in the freezing air. "Do you know her too?"

"I grew up with her. She lives next door but one."

She had stopped by the gate. When he looked at her she was looking at the ground. After a pause she said, in a different voice, "Susannah Gold could be a model, I think. I mean, she's the prettiest girl I've ever seen."

Harry felt as if a curtain had come down in front of him, which would forever prevent him from explaining some things, however hard he tried.

"She's – yes, I suppose she's all right," he began, "but—"

"Look, it's too cold to stand around here. Haven't you got any gloves, or a scarf? We're going to Chesterhill, but we can go through Lowth Heath."

"Are you sure?"

"Of course. You'll freeze, waiting for a bus. Mummy won't mind."

The reason he got into the car with her, he told himself later, was simple. Of course he didn't want to be introduced to "Mummy", and make Mrs Harding go out of her way to take him home. Of course he knew Louise was only offering him a lift because she couldn't very well avoid it. But if he *hadn't* accepted the offer, he would have done more than kicked himself. He would have beaten himself up and left himself for dead.

Mrs Harding had shiny dark hair cut shorter than her daughter's, and an accent he couldn't identify.

"Hello," she said pleasantly. Australian? No, that wasn't quite it. "Let your friend sit in the front seat, please, Louise."

Louise opened the back door obediently. The interior of the car was so dark Harry could hardly see her. He sat in the passenger seat and pulled the door, relieved that her mother hadn't called him "your young man" or something even more shaming.

"This is very kind of you, Mrs Harding."

She smiled. Apart from the hair, she didn't look much like Louise. "Well, it's so cold tonight." She spoke over her shoulder to her daughter. "You're out very late, aren't you? If rehearsals are going to go on this long we'll have to think about changing Mr Alexander's time."

"Music teacher," said Louise to Harry.

"Do you still go riding as well as doing music?" he asked, though he knew she didn't. Mrs Harding gave a snort of laughter.

"Certainly not," said Louise, beginning to laugh too. "I was awful at it. Much worse even than Susannah Gold, and that's saying something!"

Mrs Harding was still chuckling. "Susannah's a smashing blonde, but when you speak to her, she's impossible."

"She does tend to talk a lot," said Harry.

"Harry knows her," explained Louise. "They live near each other."

"Of course they do! She's at St Ursula's, isn't she? Her mother's charming."

He puzzled over the accent. When she'd said

"do" it sounded like "diu".

"Miss Drew had to bawl us out tonight, Mummy," said Louise's voice from the shadows. "She was nearly in tears, we were so awful."

"But there's plenty of time, isn't there?" said Mrs Harding optimistically. "Over a month, surely?"

"I think Miss Drew could do with some help," said Louise. "We need some training. Some proper acting classes, from a professional. I wonder if she knows any actors who might give us a master class?"

The obvious idea sprang into Harry's mind, but he jettisoned it immediately. It was ludicrous to think that Simon could teach a master class. Even though, as Harry had seen, he knew a lot about acting and could still do it perfectly well.

"You could mention it to her, I suppose."

Mrs Harding knew how to get to Lowth Heath, but Harry had to direct her to his street. When they pulled up in front of the house and he prepared to get out, Louise leaned over, undoing her seatbelt, and clasped the back of the passenger seat.

"Do you know a pizza restaurant called Tonio's?"

He wondered if Mrs Harding was really looking for something in the map pocket, or had turned away because she had seen his face in the light from the streetlamp outside Emma's bedroom window. He tried to look unaffected by Louise's small smile, half-hidden by her scarf.

"I usually go there on Fridays," he said.

"I'm sometimes there on Thursdays."

Thursday was the night he had to go to Simon's.

He opened the door. "I'd better go in."

"Tomorrow's Thursday, isn't it? I'll probably be there tomorrow," she said.

He thought this was brave, in front of her mother. Perhaps her mother wasn't like other mothers.

"Well – all right, then. Thanks for the lift," he said to Mrs Harding, who nodded and smiled widely, showing her teeth, which made her look prettier.

"Run into the house, now. Don't get cold," she told him, and he shut the car door. Louise waved from the back seat as they drove off, and Harry stood on the pavement until the car turned the corner. Then his knees weakened and he had to lean on Emma's lamppost.

Harry's father was a sales manager. He used to be a sales representative, driving around with the back of his estate car crammed with boxes of toiletries and cosmetics, which Harry had always been too embarrassed to acknowledge. He used to say his dad was something in an office, if anyone asked.

And now he was. He'd been promoted and wasn't on the road any longer, but the new job seemed much harder, and took up more hours. He worked at home, too, staring at charts and working out calculations on the computer. His eyes looked red in the mornings.

"You should get more sleep, David," said his mother.

It was Thursday morning. Four days to books-down. Harry was learning his lines at the breakfast table.

Dad reached for the sugar bowl. "How can I? Is it my fault they won't employ an assistant for me?"

"As long as you go on doing all the work of *course* they won't employ an assistant," retorted Mum. Logically, Harry thought.

"Give it a rest, Kate."

She gave it a rest, but unwillingly. Emma caught on to the unsettled atmosphere and trailed her mother round and round the kitchen, saying she didn't want to go to school because the other children were horrible to her.

"I'm not surprised," muttered Harry.

"What did you say?" Dad's eyes – the same eyes as Emma's, but with bushier eyebrows – glowered at him, his cup of tea halfway to his mouth. "Did you say I'm not surprised?"

"Dad—"

"Don't be rude to your sister." He took a gulp of tea but didn't seem to enjoy it much. "Especially when you think she can't hear it. That's a coward's insult."

"So I'm a coward!" said Harry, giving his father the sort of shrug that would have guaranteed detention from Mr Mitchell.

"Where are your manners this morning, Harry?" asked Mum.

She had turned from the sink, looking much crosser than she needed to. "It's that play, David," she said to his father. "Stardom has gone to his head."

"Don't talk rubbish." Now he'd started being rude, Harry couldn't stop. "It's just a play, for God's sake. Why does everyone go on about it all the time?"

Mum blinked at him in astonishment, the dish-cloth in her hand. "If you could only hear *yourself* going on about it! I feel sorry for poor Mr Schofield – he must be as sick of hearing about this damned play as we are."

"Don't bring Simon into this." Harry had flushed, but his voice was steady. "At least he's interested in what I'm doing, which is more than you lot are. You wouldn't care if I never did anything."

His brain felt as hot as his face. When he looked down at Malcontent's words, which he'd high-lighted in yellow, he couldn't see them properly. He shut the book and stood up.

"So you think that gives you an excuse to be cruel to Emma, do you?" asked Dad. "Talk about putting on the agony!"

Harry strongly resented it when Dad made fun of teenagers. Not many years ago he'd been far funnier than Harry could ever aspire to be. They'd often laughed together over a photo of him, in a headband and purple flared trousers, taken outside a tent at a *rock festival,* of all things, with his arm around a girl with the rattiest hair and stupidest expression Harry had ever seen.

But now he was his dad, and Harry was in enough trouble without reminding him that he'd once put on his own agony. As he left the kitchen with the playscript in his blazer pocket he heard Emma ask again, more plaintively this time, whether she had to go to school today.

"You spoil that child," said his father.

"*I* spoil her!"

Harry shut the door.

On the bus he sat down in his favourite seat, halfway along the upstairs aisle on the pavement side, and rubbed a spyhole in the steamed-up window.

He was supposed to be at Simon's at seven o'clock. He wanted to go. He wanted to see the press-cuttings, and he might even mention Louise's suggestion that someone come and teach them how to act.

But Louise had more or less invited him to meet her at Tonio's. He'd be a fool not to go, and Simon would be the first to tell him so. But how could he let him know? He'd never noticed a phone in the white room. Simon had never described how he used one, and he certainly hadn't given him a number.

He'd have to go round there early and explain. Simon was bound to understand, and say "Good man!" or something. Harry stifled the guilt caused by the thought of him sitting alone looking at the black square in the wall. Fate had intervened. And Simon of all people knew about fate.

"Monkey!" he heard suddenly from the back seat of the bus. He turned round.

"Monkey, monkey, monkey!" again, followed by ape sounds and underarm scratching. He turned back. It was only some kids fooling around. They were probably acting out some stupid new TV cartoon.

Squeals of laughter and more pushing than usual followed him down the stairs and off the bus The boys ran past him, hoo-hoo-hooing and swinging their arms.

"Bananas for breakfast, Pritchard?" called the bravest one.

"Get lost," was the best Harry could do.

His bewilderment was congealing into fear, pooling at the bottom of his stomach. If this was some new Fox offensive it would only be a matter of minutes before the man himself turned up to review the troops. And, he noticed with a shock-wave, this morning of all mornings Mr Mitchell wasn't at his post.

"Hey, Pritchard! Monkey-features! Monkey, monkey, monkey!"

There it was, the donkey's bray.

The tips of Harry's fingers began to tingle. The tingling spread up his arms and into his chest. But it wasn't cold, he realized with surprise and satisfaction. It wasn't even fear. It was anger.

He'd been angry enough at breakfast to be rude to his family. Guilt at having to share himself between Louise and Simon had made him angrier still. And if someone had to receive the result of all that anger, it might as well be Brig Fox.

His feet crunched across the frosty grass until he reached the corner of the field that was out of sight of the school building. Among the frozen cigarette stubs and crisp packets, he stopped.

There was silence. The crunching of everyone else's feet had stopped too. Brig Fox and his usual threesome were there. The kids from the bus were there. One or two curious onlookers had tagged along too. Harry put down his bag and kicked it aside.

"We'll see who's the monkey, shall we?"

Miss Drew had told him how to put evil into his voice. Keep it low, Harry, and say the ends of the words clearly. Spit it out, as though having the words in your mouth disgusts you. Go on, that's it.

Brig's expression changed. He took a step back.

"What's the matter?" asked Harry in his Malcontent voice. "*Scared?* Scared of a *monkey*? Well, I'm not scared of a *fox*!"

The crowd laughed nervously. More boys had arrived, and some girls.

"Mon–key, mon–key, mon–key!"

The chant began softly and got louder. Brig's sidekicks started it, but then more and more people joined in. No one seemed to want to champion Harry. The fact that his friends had abandoned him had never been so apparent. Suddenly he was angry with them, too. For being his friends, then suddenly deciding not to be.

He looked around. Phil Capper, the one who was always calling him a dork, was there. Roland Fox, Brig's brother, who was in the same class as Stolz and Mig, was there. He couldn't see Stolz or

Mig, though.

He took two strides across the grass and pushed Brig with all his strength. He was taller than Brig, and furious. Brig went down like a skittle. The crowd roared. Harry sat on him, pinning him down with long arms and legs, swearing loudly. Brig's bright, rodent eyes burned up at him, alight with fear and fury. His face was pale and he breathed noisily. Harry could see up his nose and inside his wet, red mouth. Brig had unnaturally straight teeth, like someone in a toothpaste advertisement. Harry pushed his fist at them. He felt like Indiana Jones.

But he hadn't been in a fight since he was nine years old. His rage had given him strength but he had no stamina. He had no back-up and no dirty tricks. Brig had plenty of both.

Within seconds the troops descended on him. He was dragged off and sent crashing face-down on the stone-hard ground. Pain started up in several parts of his body, but before he could draw breath they were on him again like demented jackals, pulling him round on to his back. And all the time they were shouting, "Mon–key! Mon–key!"

Why? What monkey-like thing had he done?

He closed his eyes as someone's boot landed under his ribs. Desperately, he rolled onto his front and tried to stay there. Three, four blows landed on his back and side. He pulled up his legs and lay on his right side, covering his head with his arms. He didn't plead, though. Indiana Jones would never plead. He clenched his teeth and waited for death or rescue.

Through the chanting he heard an unexpected voice. It wasn't Mr Mitchell. It wasn't the look-out. It was a girl, screaming.

It was Patsy O'Donnell.

Harry had only heard such screams performed by actresses in horror movies. But the real thing, Patsy-style, was far scarier.

"Get off him!" she bellowed. "Get off him! You stupid bozos, you'll kill him!"

The fight hadn't brought any teachers, but Patsy's screams couldn't fail to. It took perhaps thirty seconds for the field to empty, and when Harry opened his eyes he saw Patsy on her knees beside him, her hair curling out from under a woolly hat, and Mr Quigley, the PE teacher, fast approaching across the field.

"For God's sake, Pritchard!" said Patsy in much stronger than usual Irish. "Sure you'd have been dead if I hadn't come along!"

She helped him stand up. There was a hole in the knee of his trousers and his coat was wet through. He was bruised and in pain, but no one had aimed between his legs. Be grateful for small mercies, Mum always said.

"Look at your face. Miss Drew'll have a fit!"

Harry couldn't speak. He was glad Patsy was there.

"What happened, Pritchard?" asked Mr Quigley, looking very worried.

When Harry didn't answer he turned to Patsy. "Did you see what happened?"

She picked up Harry's bag. "No, sir."

"Now look, Patsy." Mr Quigley made an I-wasn't-born-yesterday face. "If Pritchard's been attacked by someone, Mr Mitchell will have to know."

At last Harry found some breath. "I started it, sir. It's my own fault."

Mr Quigley was doubtful. "That's hard to believe. You're not usually one of our fighters, are you?"

"Not usually, sir."

"Well." Mr Quigley seemed at a loss. He looked at Harry suspiciously. "Where does it hurt?"

"Ribs, sir. And my knee, a bit."

Mr Quigley looked down at Harry's torn trousers. He sighed and raised his eyebrows. "All right. But you're in no shape to play football this afternoon. You'd better spend Games in the library."

Together they walked back to school. Outside the locker room Mr Quigley left them, telling Harry to wash his face and comb his hair before he went to class.

"Yes, sir."

Patsy gave him his bag. "Are you all right, d'you think?" she asked.

"Yes. Thanks for what you did. I – I'm not much of a hero."

"Don't thank me. Thank those hooligans and their stupid chanting. I could hear it a mile off, and if Mitchell had been at the gate..."

"Did you hear what they were chanting?"

"Of course. They were calling you monkey.

Surely you know that?"

Harry wished there was somewhere he could sit down. His legs seemed to have disappeared. He leaned against the wall. "Do you know why? Why they were calling me monkey, I mean?"

"Why do you think?" She looked at him with blue, troubled eyes. "Pritchard, you idiot! It's this job of yours, visiting that poor crippled man. Don't you know that monkeys are trained to help people who are paralyzed, by running around the room fetching things, and picking up the phone and so on? That's what you do, isn't it?"

Weakly, Harry nodded. He could feel the blood draining away from his face.

"Well, there you are, then."

She gave him a look which he couldn't interpret. It was almost a Susannah-smile, toothy and bland. But her eyes contained a knowing, complicated expression. "I think you're doing a grand job, and good luck to you. But Fox's cronies haven't enough brain to see it like that. To them you're just the old man's monkey. D'you see?"

Harry nodded again.

"Well, you'd better get in there and smarten up, like Quigley says." She looked doubtfully at the swelling on his cheekbone. "See you in rehearsal."

The locker room was empty. Harry was late for class. He sat down on a bench and examined his grazed knee. Nothing much. It hurt to breathe, though. When he slid his hand inside his blazer to get his comb his shirt felt damp with sweat.

How had the *entire school* found out about Simon?

He pictured Tonio's. He saw himself and Susannah sitting at the counter. He remembered his dismay when she betrayed that she knew he visited an old man and his relief when he realized she didn't know that Simon was disabled.

Mum had respected his unspoken desire to keep Simon's tragedy away from gossiping neighbours. But if Susannah didn't know, then Stolz or Mig didn't know either, and they couldn't have talked about it in their classroom for Roland Fox to overhear.

He felt very cold, and shivered. Patsy knew. Patsy was Louise's friend. So did that mean that Louise knew? If so, would she think visiting Simon was a dorkish thing to do? He rested his head uncomfortably on the tiled wall, feeling as if he were about to vomit his breakfast.

Again, he pictured Tonio's. Himself and Louise sitting at one of the little marble tables. No one else in the place. He saw her go over to the jukebox. He saw himself watching her put the coins in the slot and ponder over her selection. Her hair would fall across her cheek and she'd push it back. She'd be wearing jeans. He'd never seen her in jeans.

Patsy was right. Simon was a crippled old man. By anyone's reckoning, Harry should be with a girl in a café, not with an old man in a stuffy room.

Slowly he stood up and went into the toilets. The mirror showed him the worst. On his right cheekbone a reddish-purple bruise was spreading to his eye socket. A graze on his temple had begun to throb. The whole of that side of his face looked ugly and swollen. There was mud on his nose, and on the collar of his shirt.

As he bent over the basin to splash water on his face his resentment burst out of control. It felt hot inside him, like an unerupted volcano. He remembered how furious he'd felt with Mum, that day in the kitchen. Mr Schofield's mind is sharper than yours or mine, she'd said. He's so *interesting*, Harry.

Disbelieving, Harry had implored Dad to make her see some sense. But I'll pay you, Dad had said. In notes. And Harry, hating himself for giving in to such unsubtle pressure, had agreed.

But that didn't mean he *liked* being at the mercy of adults, did it? It was true that Simon *had* turned out to be interesting, and Harry had pleased Mum by telling her so. But since the instant that Patsy's explanation had landed on his ears, with no less force than Fox's boot on his ribcage, a harsher, more immediate truth had revealed itself.

He knew now, with unshakeable conviction, that as soon as he could get off Emma duty at five o'clock, he would go and call on Simon and tell him he had something else to do, tonight and every night. He'd make him understand, somehow, that he wasn't prepared to get beaten up because of a crippled old man.

His face had no colour but the bruise. Even when tonsillitis had kept him off school for two weeks his skin hadn't looked so pale or felt so clammy. His mouth felt very dry, so he drank some water from the tap, despite the familiar scribbled-on sign above the wash basins saying NOT DRINKING WATER.

He dried his hands and face at the hot air drier, and combed his hair. For once, he decided, he would assert himself. For once he wouldn't do what people who thought they had power over him wanted. He would act like a person instead of a puppet.

He would face Simon without flinching, and tell him that he just didn't want to be his monkey any more.

BRUISED

"Has my clock stopped, or is it really only a quarter past five?"

"I've had to come early tonight," said Harry.

Simon turned from the window, smiling. Then he saw Harry's face. "Good God, what happened to you?"

He didn't sit down. "I was in a fight."

"Has your mother seen you?" Simon whizzed towards him, frowning, concerned.

"No. She only got in just as I left the house. I would have come earlier, but it's Emma. I had to stay. And I had to peel the potatoes. I do that on Thursdays."

Why couldn't he talk properly? Simon didn't want to hear all this drivel about Emma and potatoes. He tried to concentrate.

"Did someone kick you in the head?"

The anxiety in Simon's voice made Harry impatient. "No. Look, I'm all right. Just don't go on, will you?" He sat down gingerly in the armchair. His body protested. It took a superhuman effort not to wince.

"It seems to me that you didn't do much fighting." Simon was looking at him with sympathy, but it was scornful sympathy.

Harry's impatience increased. What was Simon trying to do? Humiliate him further? Well, that was easy for him, from the safety of his wheelchair.

"All right, then, I didn't. It was about thirty to one, all yelling, and about six of them kicking me." Saying this stirred the bitterness which had lain inside him all day. It swirled up. He couldn't control it. Like Malcontent, he spat out the words as if they were poisoning him. "And they were doing it because of *you*. It wasn't my fault, it was *yours*."

They looked at each other. Harry tried to quieten his breathing.

"*My* fault, you say. Well, that's interesting."

This reply was too rational for Harry. He wanted Simon to be as angry as he was. He got up and walked to the centre of the room. For the first time he noticed that he had no shadow.

"I hate these bloody lights," he said. "Do you know that? I hate them!"

Simon was surprised, but his face betrayed no bewilderment or irritation.

"I'm sorry about that. But I like them, and I spend many more hours in this room than you do."

Harry turned away. Half of him wanted to run, as usual. But the other half needed to stay and tell Simon what he had to know. He turned back.

"Why are you making this difficult for me?"

Simon raised his eyebrows. "*I'm* not doing anything! You're the one who's getting yourself into a state. You're in pain, Harry. Sit down and calm yourself."

"Why are you being so – " he cast round for an appropriate word – "so *pleasant*?"

"Would you like me to apologize? I was merely—"

"Do you know what they call me at school?"

"Henry Pritchard, I should think."

"They've started to call me monkey."

"Monkey?"

"Yes, monkey. It's a nice nickname, isn't it?"

"Why should they call you that?" At last, Simon was bewildered.

Harry indicated the roomful of gadgets. "Look," he demanded. "You've got all this, and you still need a *monkey* to run around after you!"

The bewilderment on Simon's face turned to shock. Harry's head ached and his eyeballs burned, but he couldn't make himself stop. He was like the boys who'd kicked him, over and over again. He had his victim on the ground.

"The trouble with you, Simon, is that you've been in that chair so long, with people falling over themselves to pity you and be nice to you, you've forgotten what real life's like."

Simon said nothing. His face had gone very white.

"In real life people get beaten up. People get made to look complete fools." Harry lowered himself into the computer chair. "That's what you've done to me. And I won't be your monkey – or anybody's – any more."

There was a long silence. Harry looked at the blank computer screen. He felt exhausted, as if he'd run up twenty flights of stairs.

He heard Simon's chair buzz, and when he looked round he was at the window, looking into the darkening garden.

"Is this what you came round early for?" he asked. "To tell me this?"

Harry's brain felt as blank as the screen, but with an effort he mustered his thoughts. "Yes." There was no point in mentioning Louise now.

"I see."

Harry waited. There was a long silence.

"You'd better get out of my sight, then, hadn't you?" said Simon at last.

The door to the hall was still open. The pain in Harry's side stopped him from hurrying towards it. He knew Simon was watching his reflection in the window as he hobbled across the room.

Neither of them said goodbye.

Maggie tilted his chin towards the light. She did it gently, but Harry drew in his breath sharply. He was sure Indiana Jones had never suffered this sort of pain.

"You been fightin'?"

"It looks like it."

Tonio came over and inspected the damage too.

"Your mama seen this?"

"No."

Harry hadn't gone home after he'd left Simon's. Emma would tell Mum and Dad about his blackening eye and the grazes on his face. But what could they do now? They didn't know that he'd hung around in the amusement arcade until it was late enough to go to Tonio's, with enough money in his pocket to buy pizzas for himself and Louise. And even if they suspected, what could they do?

He felt ill. He didn't want any pizza. "Can I just have a cup of tea, Tonio?"

He sat down at the table in the corner by the jukebox. He was shaking. He gripped the side of the table with both hands. It was nerves. He was nervous because Louise might come in. It wasn't anything to do with what had happened at Simon's. He tried to put Simon out of his mind.

Maggie put down his tea. In the saucer were two white pills. "You take aspirin," she said. "Then you go home an' go bed."

"Thanks."

Tonio was watching him suspiciously over the bar. "You get your head kicked?"

Why did everyone keep asking him that? Did he look as if he was going crazy?

"No, I got pushed over and the ground was very hard. I think that's when my face got hurt."

"You take those pills, like Maggie say. You want that I phone your parents?"

"No!" He slopped some tea in the saucer. "No,

it's all right, Tonio. I'm fine. I'm – I'm supposed to meet someone here."

Tonio made a clicking sound with his tongue and rearranged some glasses. He said something in Italian to Maggie, who nodded and looked in Harry's direction.

"We keep our eyes on you, Harry," said Tonio.

Harry didn't care what they did. He drank his tea slowly, trying to blot out the awfulness of the day. Just when things had started to go right. Just when Louise had offered him a lift, and actually *invited* him to meet her here. Well, almost.

The door opened noisily and Mig came in. When he saw Harry he stopped, surprised. Then he came over and sat at his table. "You're famous, mate. Did you have to go and see Mitchell?"

"No."

Mig raised his eyebrows and whistled. "Why not? Everyone who gets in a fight has to go and see him. He's like a tiger if he catches you."

"He didn't send for me," said Harry. "He wasn't at the gate this morning. Perhaps he was away. Perhaps he's ill."

"Mitchell can't get ill." He turned and signalled to Maggie. "He's a non-humanoid android."

"I think he's all right."

"Stolz saw the fight. He said he was scared when you pushed Brig over. He didn't know you could look like that."

Harry nearly smiled, but an electric shock of pain made him change his mind.

"Don't keep calling it a fight, Mig. I just got beaten up, that's all."

"Rubbish! You were all over him until the pack joined in. If they'd left it to him instead of turning on you, *he'd* be the one with the black eye."

Harry knew this wasn't true. His discomfort, mental and physical, increased.

"We got Roland Fox afterwards, you know," said Mig with satisfaction.

"Who did?" Harry swallowed one of the aspirins with a gulp of tea.

"Me and Stolz. Stolz can be quite aggressive when he's got a grievance. Well, it was all Fox's fault, wasn't it? Roland Fox, I mean."

Harry swallowed the other aspirin. "What are you talking about, Mig?"

"The fight. If Roland Fox hadn't told his obnoxious brother about you visiting that cripple, none of that monkey business would have started."

The room seemed to slide to one side. Harry blinked, and it righted itself.

"Are you all right, mate?" asked Mig. "Look, hadn't you better go—"

"How did Roland Fox know about Simon?"

"Who's Simon?"

"The old man I visit."

"Well..." Maggie brought Mig's drink. "The usual, please," he said to her, "with extra cheese." Harry's nausea rose again. "What was I saying?"

"About Roland Fox. Don't start that Coke until you've told me."

Mig put down the glass. "Well, it turns out his mum's a nurse. No, not a nurse, a sort of helper..."

"A care assistant?" Harry's mother's words.

"A care assistant. Your friend Simon—"

"He's not my friend."

"All right. This man you visit, anyway. He goes to some sort of home..."

"A day centre?"

"OK, a *day centre*, on Wednesday afternoons, and Fox's mum works there. He told her about you visiting him. Well, she must have told Roland and he told Brig and you know the rest. We got Roland for it, though. The whole monkey thing was his idea, apparently, not Brig's at all."

"What did you do?" asked Harry faintly. It had never occurred to him that *Simon* might be the source of the leak.

"At lunchtime we all bought a banana each – about twenty of us – and got him in the toilets and made him eat them all. Every single one. He was green." Mig grinned. "It was great."

"*Twenty* of you?"

"Yep," said Mig through his first sip of Coke. "Loads of us in our class – everyone hates Roland Fox – and some others as well. People in the play."

Harry let out a groan. The play. What would happen when Brig and his brother found out that he had to swing across the stage on a trapeze? He shut his eyes.

"Are you all right?" asked Mig anxiously.

He opened his eyes. "Did you know any of them?

The people in the play?"

"Not by name. Year Elevens and Twelves, mostly."

"Girls, or just boys?" he ventured, his heart climbing.

Mig gazed at him calmly. "We were in the boys' toilets, Harry."

They sat in silence for a while. Tonio's was starting to fill up. People were coming in in twos and threes, stamping their feet and uncurling scarves. Every time the door opened Harry's heart began a tap dance. Every time, it wasn't her.

Mig's pizza came. Harry watched him salt and pepper it and pick up the first slice. "What are you doing here on a Thursday night anyway, Harry?"

He had to look away from the sight of Mig talking and chewing at the same time. "I just thought I'd come in, to get away from my folks. I had a bit of a row with them this morning."

This morning's display of bad behaviour seemed primitive when he considered how spectacularly rude he'd been to Simon. Suffocating the memory, he took some coins from his pocket. "Here you are, Mig. Put some music on. I think I'd better not move."

Mig put some music on. He came back and finished his pizza. Maggie asked Harry how he felt, looked doubtful and took Mig's plate away. Mig had another Coke and put more music on. Harry ordered an espresso but when it came he found he couldn't drink it. It was twenty past nine.

He wanted to disappear. He wanted to dig a

hole in the floor and get into it, and for the floor to close up again exactly as it was before. Mig wouldn't even remember he'd been there. No one at home would miss him. He would just quietly disappear.

She hadn't come.

He tried to think. It must be because of the fight. Patsy had told her how she, Patsy, had rescued him. Whatever Louise had thought of him last night when she'd leaned towards him out of the darkness, she'd changed her mind now. And, regardless of what Dad was always saying about fickle females, he was sure she'd never change it back.

Girls despised boys who had to be rescued. Heroes in fairy stories were supposed to rescue the princesses. It was never, ever the other way round. He began a sigh, but it hurt too much to go on with.

"Why don't you go home?" suggested Mig. "Come on, I'll go with you."

"And stay with me while my folks beat me up all over again?"

Mig looked worried. "Harry, your dad's never laid a finger on you."

"Joke, Mig. They'll ground me for a fortnight, that's all."

Mig's face puckered as if he was in pain too. "Look, do you want to go home or not?"

"Nope."

"Well, what are you going to do? Sit here all night? What time have you got to be in?"

Harry felt confused, like he sometimes did in Mr

Mitchell's maths lessons, when his brain missed a step in some logical sequence, and left him reeling. "What day is it today?"

"Thursday," said Mig, bewildered.

"Does that mean it's a school day tomorrow?"

Mig's bewilderment deepened. "Yes. Look, are you sure..."

"Ten o'clock, then."

Mig looked at his watch, his face clearing. "We'll just get there by then if we go now."

"You thin' I can't get home by mysel'?" said Harry, imitating Maggie.

He felt lightheaded, a bit drunk. He had a strong urge to stand up and laugh loudly, or belch, or worse.

Mig picked up Harry's bill. "Come on, mate. Let's get home before you collapse."

They got up. Harry was very slow. His body had stiffened into a cumbersome mass which wouldn't obey instructions. He felt like a battery-operated machine without any batteries. Mig, though he was a head shorter, let him lean on him.

Tonio wouldn't take any money for Harry's drinks. "And I don't want to see you in here tomorrow," he told him. "You not fit for nothing."

"I not fit for nothing," Harry said to Mig as they emerged into the freezing dampness of the street.

"Have you got enough money for a taxi? I can't get you home on the bus in this state."

They spent Harry's pizza money on the fare, and when they got to the house Mig helped him out of the taxi.

"Thanks, mate," he said. "And thank Stolz too, for what he did to Fox's horrible brother. If I don't see him tomorrow, I mean."

Mig sucked in his breath through his teeth. "Jeez, Harry, you're not going to see anyone tomorrow except a doctor."

The front door opened before they got there. In the rectangle of light stood Mum and Dad and Emma, crowded together like a refugee family.

"Where the hell have you been?" asked Dad.

Mum put her hand over her mouth as Harry came into the light. Emma began to cry, and Razzle took advantage of the commotion to slip into the warm.

"Thanks again." Harry clapped Mig weakly on the shoulder of his padded coat. With a brief nod to Harry's parents he made off into the dark. Wisely, Harry thought.

He wouldn't let any of them help him into the house. Emma was still crying. He sat down wearily in the corner of the sofa, his chin sinking to his chest. He wanted to go to sleep.

"Well?"

Harry was eight years old again, but Dad's voice wasn't coaxing.

"Emma, go upstairs," said Mum.

Emma was leaning against the door frame, sniffing, staring at her unrecognizable brother with pink-rimmed eyes. Razzle, who had been gathered roughly into her arms, clawed the front of her dressing-gown. "I'm not sleepy. What's happened to Harry?"

"Emma, go *upstairs*," repeated Mum. "You can

take Razzle with you. And shut your bedroom door."

"But—"

"This is Harry's business. Now go upstairs and stay there."

"But you're all in here. Why can't—"

"Emma!"

She obeyed Dad. He and Mum looked at each other, then back at Harry. Mum shut the door and sat beside Harry on the sofa.

"Now," said Dad. "Explain yourself."

"What do you want to know?"

Simon must have got in touch with them, though he couldn't imagine how. Or perhaps Mr Quigley had told Mr Mitchell about the fight, and Mr Mitchell hadn't honoured their agreement. He couldn't control the trembling in his limbs. His throat ached.

"Don't give me that," said Dad, his patience thinning.

Miserably, Harry raised his head. "I was in a fight."

"That's obvious. You've worried your mother to death. Who did this to you?"

"I did it to myself. I started it. But there were too many of them."

"*You* started it?" This was Mum. "Why?"

"I don't know."

Dad was sitting on the arm of a chair with his feet on the seat and his shoes off. He sat like that sometimes when there was a penalty shoot-out on TV.

"We're not going to punish you," he said quietly. "You've been punished enough by the boy you were stupid enough to pick a fight with. But is something happening that we don't know about?"

Harry said nothing.

"If you're being bullied," said Dad, "you must tell us."

Harry still said nothing. The pain in his throat was almost unbearable. He hadn't cried since he fell out of a tree and sprained his ankle, more than two years ago.

"You must tell us," repeated Dad.

"I can't." His voice was a whisper.

"Why not?" asked Mum. She was almost crying too.

"I made a pact."

"Who with?"

"Mr Mitchell, the deputy head. He takes me for maths. He said he'd give me until the end of term to deal with this, or he'll tell my parents. He trusts me, so why can't you?"

They looked at each other, and Harry looked at each of them.

"Please."

Mum squeezed his hand. The fight against tears intensified.

"But if people are beating you up, Harry..." began Dad.

"They're not. I mean they won't any more."

Dad sighed. He stood up and looked down at Harry from under his wiry eyebrows. When he spoke again his voice was still worried, but less suspicious. "This Mr Mitchell knows who the bullies are, does he?"

Harry nodded.

"And he's got his eye on them?"

Harry nodded again.

"Well, then."

He looked at Mum. Harry looked at her too. Her tears had nearly come, and she struggled to control them. He heard the strain in her voice. "I don't know what to say, David."

Dad had sat down again on the arm of the chair. He turned the signet ring on his little finger round and round, which he always did when he was thinking. "What about going along with this teacher for now?" he said to her. "He must know what he's doing."

Mum's shoulders stiffened. She looked soulfully at Dad. "But the parents should know what their sons are doing! If Harry were a bully, you'd want to know, wouldn't you?"

Dad sighed. Mum's reasonableness, by which he and Harry were regularly defeated, defied opposition. "Of course I would. But if this teacher believes Harry can sort it out himself..."

"I can, I *can* sort it out," said Harry. He leaned forward, cradling his right elbow in his left hand. His face seemed to be nearer the carpet than usual. "I've already started to – to sort it out."

There was a silence. Mum put her hand on his knee. Silently, he prayed. But whoever he prayed to didn't hear him.

"You've been at Mr Schofield's house all evening, haven't you?" Mum's voice was soft, but it had a little edge to it.

Harry grunted, trying again to swallow the lump in his throat.

"Emma told us that you met her from school with your face in that state, and you changed out of your uniform and disappeared the minute you heard my car. Here."

She gave him a tissue. Blowing his nose gave him time to decide what to say, though he scarcely had the breath to say it.

"I haven't been there all evening..."

"You still haven't told us where you *have* been," interrupted Dad.

"I've been at Tonio's. I'd arranged to meet someone there, and couldn't see Simon at seven o'clock." The pain in his chest increased, but he struggled on. "I had to – I had to go round early to give him the message. I couldn't phone him, could I?"

"Why not?" said Mum. "He has a special hands-free phone. You should have asked me."

"Oh." Harry felt defeated.

"And was he all right about not seeing you tonight?" asked Dad. "Not disappointed?"

"No, I don't think so." An ungenerous thought came to him. "He's had bigger disappointments in his life."

They didn't know about the quarrel, then. Harry waited, breathing as shallowly as possible. Hidden by his jeans, the graze on his knee under Mum's hand began to burn. He wanted very much for this inquisition to end. He wanted to lie down and go to sleep for a hundred years.

Mum's fingers tightened slightly. He winced, but both her grip and her voice were insistent. "This stupid fight at school's got something to do with Mr Schofield, hasn't it?"

Harry pushed her hand away. "No."

"Look, Harry." Dad hitched up his trousers and knelt on the floor so that he could see Harry's face. "If Mr Mitchell can make a bargain with you, so can we. We'll agree to what he wants, though it goes against our better judgement, if you tell us what really happened at Mr Schofield's." He looked up at Mum. "That's fair, isn't it, Kate?"

"Ye – es." It was a sort of sigh.

"That's fair, isn't it, Harry?"

Harry nodded.

"Tell the truth," said Mum.

The pattern on the carpet blurred. Harry blinked vigorously. "I – I've given up my job," he said, with an effort. "They called me names about it at school. I told Simon I'm not going round to visit him again. Ever."

Mum tried to say something, but Dad suppressed her. "Is that the truth?"

"Yes." It was some of it, anyway.

Dad stood up. His voice seemed to come from miles away. "All right, then. Till the end of term. But if this name-calling and fighting nonsense is still going on next term I'll be down at that school as fast as if my pants were on fire."

"Thanks," said Harry feebly, and closed his eyes.

TRUTH

Harry had never seen Simon's house in daylight. When he'd shuffled up the steps on Thursday with pain in his ribs and rage in his heart, it had been in an icy, murky dusk.

The shrubs in the front garden were neatly tended, but the house hadn't received any care for years and years. Harry noticed that the paint was peeling and the windowpanes were very dirty. Part of the old metal gutter had come loose and dangled dangerously from the corner. A lot of slates were missing from the roof of the porch. Nervously, he pushed the bell.

It was Sunday morning.

Harry's angry Thursday had been followed by a miserable Friday. Dr Jones had announced that his ribs were badly bruised, as were his scapula, clavicle and patella.

"Shoulder blade, collar bone and kneecap," Mum had translated as she drove him home. "I've got to go to work, but I want you to do as the doctor says and stay in bed and take those pills. I've phoned school."

Harry had lain in bed in the silent house. He was so stiff it took him ages to reach the bathroom and ages to get back into bed again. But when Dr Jones's painkillers started to work he almost wished they hadn't. Not having to concentrate on the pain allowed his mind to break free again, and think.

Twin burdens of guilt and shame fell on him, squashing him flat. He lay there, unable to squirm physically, but squirming in his head, hour after hour.

What manic stupidity had driven him to cause Simon – *Simon* of all people, who didn't bully him or call him a dork or fail to turn up – such unhappiness? And how could he possibly make amends?

Mum, who cared for Simon too, had been devastated to hear that Harry had given up his job. She had insisted, her face pinched with disappointment, that he go and reinstate himself as soon as he was fit enough.

"He might not want to see me," Harry had admitted.

She hadn't asked any questions, but she had gone to the phone immediately, late on Thursday night. Dad had protested that Simon would be asleep, but Mum had shaken her head, searching for the number in her pocket-book and click-clicking it into the phone.

"He doesn't sleep well. Margaret puts him to bed at ten, but he reads for hours. He can't use much energy, so he doesn't need much sleep. Hello? Mr Schofield? It's Kate Pritchard."

Harry had waited in unbearable suspense.

But Simon hadn't let him down. Mum had said yes and no a few times and replaced the receiver. "He won't speak to you now, Harry, but he's looking forward to seeing you at the weekend. And you're *definitely* going. No choice."

So here he was. Guilt had given way to resignation by Saturday, when he'd got up and experimented with moving around. The swelling round his eye had begun to go down, and he no longer wanted to yelp every time he took a step or picked something up. On Saturday night he'd watched *Match of the Day* with Dad, to please him, and Dad had let him watch a late movie after Mum had gone to bed, which was his way of making peace. He'd stopped Harry's allowance for a week, but that was all.

He considered himself forgiven at home. But how much forgiveness would he meet with at Simon's house?

Simon was in bed. Alarmed, Harry stopped by the door. "I'm sorry – am I too early? I thought Mum arranged—"

"Just feeling a bit under the weather," said Simon. "Come in and sit down."

Harry sat down on the white wickerwork chair by the bed. He couldn't keep anxiety out of his voice. "Are you all right?"

"Oh, yes. Got a bit of a cold. Are *you* all right?"

Harry hung his head. "I'm feeling much better,

thanks. I – I'm really sorry about what happened on Thursday."

"Your dear mother said you would be."

"She doesn't know exactly what I said to you."

"I should hope not. Why give her further pain?"

There was a pause. Harry didn't know how to speak to Simon in this new situation. He was used to him whizzing about the room like a Dalek. Then he remembered something, and stood up. "Shall I get the cuttings book?"

The enthusiasm he'd expected didn't come. "No. I don't think I want to look at it today. Sit there and let's talk."

Harry sat down again, feeling uncomfortable. "What about?"

"You know very well. We've both had a couple of days to think about it. I've certainly got something to say, and I hope you have, too."

What did Simon want him to say? He'd apologized. He'd got it over with almost in his first sentence, as his mother had advised.

"Haven't you come to any conclusions?" Simon prompted.

Still Harry said nothing. He pushed back his hair, puzzled.

"Go over and look at the computer. It's all right, the microphone's off."

Harry did so. There on the screen was the message he'd seen on his first visit. NO SHADOWS.

"On Thursday you said you didn't like my lights. 'I hate these bloody lights,' you said, didn't you?"

Harry sat down by the computer. In daylight the room looked almost normal, though above the bed two spotlights burned brightly, and the standard lamp in the corner was on. "I suppose so."

"You haven't understood why I have the lights on all the time, and why the room is painted white to reflect them, have you? Has it never occurred to you to question these things?"

Harry looked up at him in the high bed. He seemed calm, but his chin was angled and his eyes bright.

"No, it hasn't," he admitted. "I'm a moron."

"You're not a moron, Harry, though occasionally you act like one."

Harry knew this was true.

"I'm going to do something I swore I'd never do," said Simon. "I'm going to ask you to put yourself in my place. Will you do it?"

Harry swallowed. "If you like."

"Go and sit in my wheelchair, then. It's over there by the window where Nurse Margaret left it this morning."

Harry hesitated.

"Go on, boy."

Miss Drew often said, "If it feels wrong, it is wrong." As he lowered himself into Simon's chair, Harry knew with overwhelming certainty that it felt wrong. But he couldn't disobey. He was manacled by his guilt as securely as a monkey on a chain.

"Comfortable?" asked Simon.

"Yes, thank you."

"Good. Relax into it. Use the headrest. And the footrest, too."

Harry obeyed.

"That's my boy. Now, sit still. Be the actor in *Whose Life Is It Anyway?* Sit as still as you can, for as long as you can. Relax, or your muscles will stiffen up."

There was a pain in Harry's stomach. The headrest and footrest of the wheelchair, adjusted to fit Simon, also fitted him. Simon's emaciated body was as tall as his own.

"Why do you want me to do this?"

Simon said nothing for a long time. Harry concentrated every fibre of his muscles on keeping absolutely still. The room was very quiet. Outside the window the garden, which he had never seen before, stretched to a rear wall covered in well-trimmed evergreens. The spotlights shone on Simon's white hair as he lay against the white pillow in the white bed. The electric clock ticked, ticked, ticked. Harry had never noticed before that electric clocks don't tock.

"If you had to live as I do," said Simon slowly, "you wouldn't want shadows in your room. You wouldn't want to look at a wheelchair shape on the floor or the wall. You'd want to see the shape of a tall man, with muscles in his arms and legs. Wouldn't you?"

"Yes," said Harry obediently.

"You may not have noticed, but there are no mirrors in this room either."

He hadn't noticed. "Can I move now?"

"No. Do you understand why there are no mirrors?"

"I think so."

"And what is your theory?"

"You don't want to see your reflection."

"Exactly. I want this room to reflect what is outside it. Books and plays, music, memories, the wonderful world of high technology. I never want to see what is inside it. A man in a wheelchair. A cripple."

Harry was silent.

"That's what I mean when I say my life is in my head. My head is glad I survived the crash; my body is not. So shadows and mirrors are not welcome here. I don't want to see myself as I am."

The pain in Harry's muscles was becoming intolerable. "Can I move now?" he asked desperately.

"Go on, then. Get out of the chair and come here."

Relieved, he tumbled out of the chair and sat on the floor. "I've got pins and needles."

Simon was looking at him with sorrow. "You're a good boy, Harry. Would you hold up my bottle of water, please?"

Simon drank quite a lot of the water. As Harry stood there by the bed a feeling crept over him. It was compassion, he decided. He was glad he was there to help Simon with his drink of water. It was the compassion of a nurse.

No it wasn't. Simon stopped sipping and Harry put the bottle back on the bedside table. It wasn't compassion. It was – insanely – a kind of envy.

For Simon's ability to find the truth, and explain it.

"So," said Simon. "Let's get back to my original question. Have you come to any conclusions about the fight?"

"I don't know."

"Even after what I've just shown you?"

Harry sat down again in the wickerwork chair. "About the shadows, you mean?"

"Exactly. Everyone's life has shadows, you know. Everyone shies away from looking at the reflection of themselves they may not want to see."

Harry said nothing.

"How long has this bullying been going on?" asked Simon softly.

As usual, it was pointless to lie. "Oh, ages."

"And is it one boy, or several?"

"One. Though he's got a few accomplices."

"And this boy, the leader. What's his name?"

"Gerard Fox. People call him Brigadier, or Brig for short."

"Because of the racehorse?"

"What racehorse?"

"There was a famous racehorse called Brigadier Gerard."

"I didn't know that," said Harry. "I've often wondered where the name came from." He glanced at Simon's face, which was looking entertained. "You must think I'm so stupid."

"Not at all. And is this fellow tall and handsome, like a racehorse?"

"*No*. He's shorter than me and – sort of wiry, but strong, and..."

"And what?"

"Well – you'll laugh."

"Try me."

"Well, I always think of him as *foxy,* somehow. His name suits him well."

"Is he clever?"

"He's good at physics."

"Is he the boyfriend of darling Louise?"

"No!" Harry's horrified stare made Simon smile.

"Well then, what possible power can he have over you?"

Harry had no answer except the obvious one. He chewed his lip.

"Could it be that you *like* being bullied?" Simon's eyes looked very blue. "Because it means you can feel sorry for yourself?"

"For God's sake, Simon..."

"For God's sake what?"

"You know that's not true."

"Isn't it? Look, you know perfectly well that bullies thrive on violence. So you pick a fight with him and get whacked for your trouble! Fight him with your *brain,* boy."

Harry's palms felt sweaty. He pressed them together, twisting his fingers.

"I can't, Simon."

"Why not? Because being bullied is so wonderful that you came round here on Thursday to show *me* what it was like?"

He was silenced. But Simon waited testily for his answer.

"I can't do it because I'm – because I'm a dork," he said at last. "Everyone at school thinks so. Everyone."

Simon paused before he spoke, breathing noisily. "I see. In other words, *you* do."

"Well, so would you," said Harry moodily, "if you really knew me."

"Don't tell me what to think." Simon's cheeks above his white beard looked pink. "And stop assuming this boy is Superman. Everyone has a weak spot. When you've found out what his is, the rest will be easy."

Harry looked doubtful, but Simon persevered. "What else can you tell me about him?"

"Not much," said Harry, thinking hard. "He's got a brother called Roland."

"Roland and Gerard! How delightfully French! Sorry. Go on."

"Roland Fox is in the year above me, in the same class as my mates Chris Stolz and Martin Easterhouse, who's always called Mig."

"But who are these people? You've just told me everyone thinks you're a dorp."

"A dork."

Harry thought about Stolz and the bananas. He thought about Mig taking him home in a taxi when the world wouldn't stay upright. He thought about his pact with Mr Mitchell, which Mum and Dad had respected too.

"All right, then. Not everyone."

"So there are plenty of people who would be pleased to see a trap laid for Fox?"

Harry smiled. His cheek hurt. "That's what Mr Mitchell does. Makes puns on his name all the time. Talks about 'running him to earth' and so on. I think he treats it as a bit of a game."

"Who's Mr Mitchell?"

"The deputy head. He's given me until the end of term, which is about five weeks. If I haven't sorted Fox out by then, he'll tell Fox's mother and an unholy fuss will break out. My parents already know some of it. But they've agreed to the pact as well."

"Excellent people, your parents."

Harry tried to look non-committal.

"This boy. The Brigadier Gerard boy. Is he in your class?" asked Simon.

"No, but I'm with him for a lot of lessons. He's in my set a lot."

"Does that mean he's good at the things you're good at?"

"Well, yes."

"So a battle of wits might interest him more than a battle of fists, and save your good looks from further injury into the bargain?"

Harry frowned unhappily. "Simon – you don't know what he's like."

The thought of engaging in a battle of wits with Fox made him sweat. "He's – he's sort of *scary*. He makes me feel so feeble and – and..."

Simon studied his face. "Unmanly?"

They looked at each other. Blushing, Harry

dropped his head. His hair flopped forward.

"Ah," said Simon with satisfaction. "You must learn to be a truth-seeker."

Harry's cheeks flamed, but he looked up. "I *am* learning. I think I see what you're getting at."

"And what is it?"

He took a few seconds to arrange his thoughts into the right order. "Well, it's all to do with Louise, isn't it?"

"It might be," said Simon. "Go on."

"I want her to like me, but girls don't like boys who are weak. The more Fox bullied me, the weaker I felt, so I expected her to hate me. But on Wednesday – the night before the fight – she was pretty nice to me. I thought maybe she liked me after all. So when Fox called me a monkey in the playground the next morning I didn't feel ... unmanly. I stood up to him because – because of her, or something. But now that's all gone wrong."

This was the longest speech he had ever made to Simon. His flush was retreating, but he dipped his head.

"How has it gone wrong?" asked Simon gently.

With difficulty Harry steadied his voice. "She was supposed to meet me at Tonio's – a pizza place we go to – on Thursday night. That's why I couldn't come and see you. But she..." He had to stop. He looked at the floor.

"She didn't turn up?" offered Simon.

He nodded.

"Well then, you've got two things on your list.

First, deal with the ape who called you a monkey. Second, deal with the dame who stood you up."

Harry's head came up fast.

"Aha!" Simon's eyes crinkled at the corners. "Listen, Harry. Girls can be a grade one nuisance, or absolutely special, or anything in between. But *all* of them will inflict unlimited misery on a man rather than be made to look foolish. And you can get the last laugh yet, you know."

Harry was interested. "How?"

"Well, by Thursday afternoon news of the fight, and the injuries you received, must have been all round school. Rather than risk being stood up herself, the lovely Louise didn't bother to go. Have you seen her since?"

"No."

"Then the way is clear for you tomorrow, my boy! She'll be dazzled to death that you didn't let her down even though you were in pain. She'll practically beg you for another date! You'll see."

Harry digested this information. "I don't believe you."

"When's your next rehearsal?" asked Simon, with a widening smile.

"Tomorrow, after school."

"And are you coming to see me later tomorrow, as usual?"

"Of course."

"Well, I expect a favourable report."

With difficulty, Harry smiled. "I'll do my best."

"How's *Accelerando* going, anyway?" asked

Simon. "You've been here all this time and we haven't mentioned it yet. Anyone would think it isn't the most important thing in our lives!"

The green numbers on Simon's clock read 12:45. Mum would be putting the roast potatoes in. Harry shoved them to the back of his mind.

"Oh, the play. It's terrible."

"Good, good. The more terrible it is at this stage – five weeks to go, did you say? – the better it'll be in the end."

"You're just saying that, Simon."

Harry tried to envisage the next five weeks. The same five weeks between now and the end of term during which he had to get Fox, learn to swing on a trapeze, memorize all his lines and moves, and do something about Louise.

"Not at all. I'll be there on the last night, you know, in my yellow cravat and spats, with an ebony cane."

Harry didn't know what spats were. But Simon was only joking anyway. "I'll get you a ticket," he said.

"Get me two. I'll bring my girlfriend."

Harry hated it when Simon said things like that. He couldn't tell if he was really bitter, or pretending to be for some reason of his own. Disgust at how badly he'd treated him welled up again.

Then he had the sort of inspiration which usually only happens long after the moment when it was needed has passed.

"Can I ask you a favour, Simon?"

"Fire away." Simon was beginning to look tired, but his blue eyes were attentive.

"Someone suggested that we – the Drama Club – could do with some proper acting tuition. From a professional. Do you think *you* might be able to do a master class for us? If we could organize transport, I mean?"

He was reddening again, though he didn't understand why he should be embarrassed. Simon's eyes looked bluer than ever. They were also a bit moist. A few moments passed before he spoke.

"I'd be honoured, Harry. Absolutely honoured."

Harry wanted to grin, but his bruised cheek only allowed him a normal-sized smile.

"Thanks. Thanks a lot." He had made the best amends possible. His flush disappeared, and unself-consciously he grasped Simon's hand as it lay on the bedcovers. "I'll speak to Miss Drew about it tomorrow."

HERO

All of a sudden February had begun to look like March. As Harry searched his pockets for his key he noticed that his mother's daffodils by the garden path were showing their yellow underwear. The sun was out and the air felt soft, though not yet warm. The moment when his face had hit that frost-hardened field seemed to have taken place in another century.

He stood on the doorstep, looking across to the Heath. Two boys and a man were trying to fly a kite. He watched them and listened to their laughter. Later, perhaps, though he wasn't up to riding his own bicycle, he might take Emma out on hers.

The smell of Sunday lunch filled the hall.

"Is that you, Harry?"

Who else would it be? Still, the first time he came in and Mum *didn't* say it, he'd know something had changed for ever.

Her face, rosy from cooking, came round the kitchen door. "Wash your hands, darling. I'm just dishing up. There was a phone call for you."

"It was a *girl*," added Emma, sliding into the cloakroom in front of him. "Not Susannah. She sounded posh. Too posh for *you*."

He controlled himself as best he could, though his stomach was churning. "Hurry up," he said to Emma. "And get out. I want to use the toilet."

When he'd finished he felt better. He tried to breathe deeply while he dried his hands. He inspected his bruised eye in the mirror. It looked terrible. Worse than it felt. He took another deep breath. His ribs hurt.

Emma and Dad were already at the table. Harry sat down and took his napkin out of its ring. He looked at his place mat. It was one of the set Mum kept for Sunday and Christmas, with the picture of grazing horses on it. When he was a little boy his favourite had been the chestnut one with the white flash on its forehead and two white socks. He straightened his knife and fork.

"Who's your girlfriend?" giggled Emma.

"Shut up," said Dad. Emma made the face which always reminded Harry of a startled squirrel, or possibly a stoat. "And go and help in the kitchen. It's about time you started to make yourself useful."

He made these commands in a soft, reasonable voice. Having no excuse for tears or protest, Emma put down her napkin and got up. When she'd left the dining room Dad rubbed his hands together and gave Harry a gleeful look. "That's the way to do it, isn't it?"

Harry, amazed, said nothing.

Mum came in with a laden plate in each hand. "How did things go at Mr Schofield's?" she asked as she put Harry's down.

"Fine. He was in bed because he's got a cold. But he's all right."

"Is that all?"

"Yes." What else could he say, without betraying more than either he or Simon would want her to know? "Honestly, it was OK. I'm going round as usual tomorrow night, and I'm going to arrange for him to come to school and talk to us about acting."

Mum paused in the doorway. "Whose idea was that?"

"Mine," said the truth-seeker. "Well, sort of."

Emma came in very slowly, carrying the gravy jug and saucer with both hands, her tongue peeping out of the corner of her mouth. As she put the jug down on the table Dad leaned across and cupped her small face in his large hand, which he only did when he was pleased. "Good girl," he said. "I expect you to be our waitress every Sunday from now on. And if you don't spill anything, I'll give you some wages."

Emma, unsure whether to be pleased or dismayed, plumped into her chair. Her freckles disappeared under a deep flush.

Mum came back with the other two plates. She sat down, then began to stand up again. "I've forgotten the mustard."

"I'll go," said Harry, putting down the knife

he'd just picked up.

"No you won't," said Dad in the same reasonable voice. "Emma, get the mustard."

Harry picked up his knife again. He cleared his throat. "Did you say there was a phone call for me, Mum?"

"Oh! I'd forgotten." She took a piece of paper from the pocket of her cardigan. "Sorry, darl – er ... here you are."

He unfolded the paper. Louise – just Louise, with no surname – followed by the time she'd phoned and the number. He recognized his mother's square writing.

"What did she say?" he asked, cutting up a carrot into very small pieces.

"*I* picked up the phone," said Emma as she put the mustard pot in the middle of the table.

Mum gave Harry a conspiratorial look. "Don't worry, I soon took over. The girl wanted to know how you were feeling. There's some concern at school about you, apparently."

"I'm not surprised," muttered Dad with his mouth full.

"What did you tell her?" asked Harry.

"I said you'd be back at school tomorrow. But she left her number and asked if you could phone her this afternoon."

"Thanks." Under the table, his knees were trembling. He tensed his muscles and pressed his feet into the carpet.

"Why does she want him to phone her if she'll

see him at school tomorrow?" asked Emma.

"Just eat, monster," said Dad.

Emma ignored him. "I bet she lives in Chesterhill, doesn't she?"

There was a silence. Suddenly, Harry couldn't stand it. He turned to Mum, and out of the corner of his eye he saw Dad look up. "They *do* live in Chesterhill. But her mother's really nice. She gave me a lift home on Wednesday, when Miss Drew kept us late after rehearsal, even though it was miles out of her way. And she knows Susannah, and Mrs Gold."

Mum was interested. "How does she know Erica?"

"Through Susannah's riding school. You know, the one we're always hearing about at great length. Louise Harding used to go there."

It was the first time he'd said her name to his parents. Talking about her was better than not talking about her, though.

"What did you say the surname is?" asked Mum.

"Harding."

Mum looked at him with her head on one side. He noticed that her face was thin and her shoulders stuck out squarely under her cardigan. Like his face, like his shoulders. She was his mum and he was glad. "Dark-haired woman, with a South African accent?"

"That's right." Of course it was South African.

"I've met her at Erica's." She looked at Dad. "She's charming, David."

"That's what *she* said about Mrs Gold," remembered Harry.

Dad laughed, and patted his mouth with his napkin. "Well, as long as the girls think each other are charming, we fellas don't have to bother to make them think we're so desirable, do we?"

Mum laughed too. "Pass the mustard, please, Emma. Oh, and when you return this girl's call, Harry, why don't you use the phone in the den?"

Mrs Harding's dark, well-polished car jerked to a halt. Harry was watching from the sitting-room window. He watched Louise get out on the pavement side and open the gate. She was wearing ironed-looking jeans and a white coat, and was carrying something in her right hand. The whiteness of the coat and the darkness of her hair splashed against each other in the sunlight. He dashed to open the front door as fast as his bruised ribs would allow.

"Hey," she said, and turned to wave to her mother. Harry waved too. The car drove away.

"Hey," he said.

"You look terrible."

"Tell me something I don't know."

He held open the door. As she stepped inside, the hall clock struck four o'clock. "Dead on time," he said.

Bashfully, her head went down and her hair came over her cheeks. Harry battled with a strong desire to touch it. He could imagine what it felt like – smooth yet textured, solid yet fluid. Proper hair, unlike his own light, babyish strands.

"Your mother believes in punctuality, I suppose," he said.

She read his face, and smiled. "My mother doesn't take me *everywhere,* you know. It's just that there aren't any buses from Chesterhill on a Sunday."

He smiled back. "Would you like to take off your coat?"

She began to, then stopped. "It's too nice today to stay indoors. Why don't we go for a walk?"

Harry added this to his huge collection of ideas he wished he'd had. "Why don't we?"

Mum was on her knees on the back lawn, weeding. She straightened up when Harry and Louise came out of the house.

"This is Louise," he said shyly. "We're going for a walk."

Louise smiled and nodded. "My mother's coming for me at six, Mrs Pritchard," she said. "We'll be back well before it gets dark." She was obviously practised at dealing with parents.

"All right, dear. Take your key, Harry."

Dear? He patted his pocket. "Got it."

They went back through the house. Louise watched him put his coat on and zip it up. "You're quite tall, aren't you?"

"Yep." He turned up his collar, feeling masculine. "It's the only thing that recommended me to Miss Drew as an actor, I think."

"Nonsense." She looked down at the small paper-bag-covered object in her hand. "Oh, I almost forgot to give you this. It's from all of us in the cast and backstage."

Harry took it.

"Get well soon," she said.

It was a box of chocolate mints. Not very big, not very expensive, but proof that Simon was right. Some people wouldn't be sorry to see Fox in a trap.

"Thanks." He put the mints back in their bag and left them on the hall table. "And thanks to the others, too."

"You'll see them at rehearsal tomorrow – books-down, remember! My lines are *atrocious*. Miss Drew's going to go spare."

They left the house. Harry pulled the door and stuck his hands in his pockets. He'd forgotten his gloves again. They crossed the road to the Heath.

"Miss Drew was a bit upset when Patsy told her you'd been hurt in a fight," said Louise.

Harry drove his hands deeper into his pockets. "Why shouldn't Malcontent have a few bruises? He's a villain, isn't he? Though they'll be gone by the first night, I suppose."

"They do look sore," she said sympathetically. "Why didn't you go straight home? You should have got them to phone your mother."

"She was at work. And to be honest, I didn't feel as bad on Thursday morning as I did later. But Quigley let me off football, which was something."

She giggled into her scarf. "You're the only boy I've ever met who doesn't like football. Most of them talk of nothing else. But if they knew how boring it is for girls they wouldn't do it." She thought for a moment. "Or maybe they would anyway."

Harry thought this was pretty likely. He was as mystified as other boys about how to talk to girls. But as he shortened his stride beside hers along one of the sandy paths, he felt that he'd been given an opportunity which may never come again.

"Did Patsy say anything else about the fight?"

The wind blew her fringe away from her forehead, revealing that she was frowning. "Well, everyone knows that it was Gerard Fox who started the name-calling. A boy in Year Eleven, Chris Stolz his name is, said that you pushed Gerard down, so I suppose you started the fight, didn't you?"

He shrugged. "I suppose I did."

She looked at him, her face clearing. Then she looked ahead again. Her hair hid her expression. After a pause she said, "You're a bit of a hero, actually."

Something warm began to trickle through his veins, right to the cold tips of his fingers and toes, like the hot milk and honey Mum gave him when he was ill. "I don't feel much like one."

"Well, I think you were pretty brave. It's about time someone sorted Gerard Fox out."

"He ended up sorting *me* out, though, didn't he?"

Her reaction was the same as Mig's had been. "That's not true!" Although it retained its usual pallor and clear, sculptured look, her face was troubled. "Everyone in the whole school is on your side against those – what does Patsy call them?"

He could think of several things Patsy had called them. "Bozos?"

"That'll do – bozos. On Friday people were talking of nothing else."

They walked on in silence for a few minutes. Harry wished he could bring up the subject of Thursday night, but it was really up to her to do so.

"How can everyone in the whole school be on my side?" he asked.

Her chin tilted. Harry's long-held conviction that she thought too much of herself flared up briefly, but he smothered it.

"I mean, there must have been about thirty of them, which is at least one classroomful," he said reasonably. "And if you suggest that I get thirty of my own thugs and take his gang on, I'm afraid I'll just have to push you into the pond."

They'd reached the pond at the lowest point of the Heath. It was small and dirty, full of rubbish and overgrown with weeds. It had been the most out-of-bounds place of all his parents' out-of-bounds places when he was little, and still was for Emma. On the opposite bank two small boys whose parents weren't so governessy were trawling for wildlife with nets and jamjars.

Louise was giggling. "You wouldn't dare."

"Just watch me."

He had never been in this situation with a girl before. He hoped, strongly, that Louise hadn't been in it with a boy. But he discovered that he could perform the whole scene without needing a script.

She backed away, her toes slipping on the muddy mess the thaw had made of the edge of the pond.

She took her hands out of the pockets of her coat and spread her arms to steady herself. The afternoon sun, lowering behind her, spun a web of wintry light round her dark hair. She was smiling.

Harry's unwritten script told him to catch her round the waist. Not too high, not too low. She didn't push him away. "Are you drowning me or saving me?" she asked, still smiling.

He could never have predicted that her body would be so slender, yet so soft. Her coat, which was made of some kind of velvety, white, expensive wool, seemed to disappear. He could feel her ribcage, and the little knobs on her spine, and her fast, tense breathing.

It lasted only a few seconds. She twisted and ran away, up the bank from the pond, her head bowed against the wind. Harry followed more slowly. His injured knee had begun to protest.

When he reached the top of the slope, Louise was sitting on a bench, her legs crossed at the ankles, her hands thrust once more into her pockets. He winced as he sat down, and tried not to gasp. She didn't look at him.

"You're wrong, you know, about Fox and his gang," she said. "Patsy saw what happened. There were only two of them – Fox and one of those three boys who are always with him. They were kicking you hard enough to kill you, she says. No one else touched you."

Harry was stunned. *Two?*

"More than two were chanting, though," he said

defensively. "That's how Patsy knew the fight was going on. She heard the crowd chanting."

She flicked her hair behind her ear with a grey-gloved hand. Harry clenched and unclenched his fists inside his pockets, watching her profile as he had done many times before. She seemed calm, but nervous at the same time. And he couldn't unravel his own feelings at all.

He had touched her. Whatever happened in the future, that fact was now history. In the secret, unspoken way girls operated, she had wanted him to, and he had done it.

"That was *chanting,* Harry. Chanting is hardly fighting. And it certainly isn't kicking a man who's down, which is just cowardice and shows what a no-brain Fox is."

He stopped looking at her. He looked at his feet and thought for a long time. Louise didn't say anything else. He knew that she would wait patiently for his answer, and listen to it when it came. For a girl, she was pretty good at doing that.

"I don't think Fox is a no-brain," he said at last. "He's like a gangster with a group of hoodlums. A sort of mastermind. He's in top set for almost everything, as well as being good at sport. And he's much better at physics than anyone else. Fatso Collier's practically in love with him, and is always saying things like 'Fox, explain to these simpletons what electro-magnetism is, will you, while I get on with something else?'"

Louise smiled, but didn't try to interrupt. Spurred on by the knowledge that his thoughts about Fox were getting clearer and clearer as he talked, Harry continued.

"Shall I tell you something else about him?"

She nodded.

"He won a poetry prize in Year Seven. He was in my class then, and I can remember our English teacher reading out his poem."

She shifted her bottom on the seat, but no nearer him. Just to get more comfortable. "That's hard to believe," she said scornfully. "What was the poem like?"

"Well, it was very good." Simon's words drummed at the back of his mind as he spoke. If he could find the truth about Fox, the act of truth-seeking might reveal some other truths, more personal and more deeply hidden.

"Can you remember what it was about?" she asked, interested.

"It was about the death of a pet dog or cat or something. Well, we were only in Year Seven. But I'm beginning to suspect that it was really about his dad, who died when he was a little kid."

Louise sat forward, hunched in her coat, half-turned towards him. There was a pause. Then her gaze landed on his face. "But if he's so clever, why is he doing something as prattish as calling you names and kicking you?"

"I don't know. Because my dad didn't die, perhaps?"

He watched her face. Her grey and green eyes glittered, and the tip of her nose was beginning to turn pink in the wintry air. The sun was a blotch of orange near the horizon. She turned and gazed at it, her small, narrow hands clasped between her knees. "So I'm supposed to feel sorry for *him*, poor tortured soul, am I?"

"No, of course not. But – I mean, if I can understand *why* he's been bullying me all these months—"

"All these months!" Her eyes had stretched. Not, he thought, in one of her actress tricks, but with genuine surprise.

"Oh, yes." He moved his leg a little bit, so that it touched her knee. Either she didn't notice or didn't mind. "But it's getting near its end now. By the time we do the play, it'll all be over."

"What are you going to do?"

"I'm going to try a bit of psychology. I'm already on the way to finding Fox's weak spot. When I've got it, I'll trap him."

She pushed back her fringe. The frown was still there, faintly, but her lips were slightly parted and her eyes were beginning a smile. The expression on his own face had escaped from his control. He didn't know if he was grinning like a hyena or gaping like a fool.

"You might be right about Fox being brainy, Harry, but you're brainier." She slid him a soft, sideways look. "And although Fox is pretty good-looking in his way, so are you. In fact you look positively *intellectual* when you've got those tortoiseshell glasses on. Patsy thinks so, too."

Harry was embarrassed and pleased at the same time. His self-consciousness when reading his lines was worsened by having to wear his glasses to do it. But he tried to shrug off the compliment, hero-style. "Tough luck tomorrow, then, girls. The glasses will be in my pocket along with the script."

Her smile had faded, and she was looking at him thoughtfully, as if something had been revealed to her. "You know," she said slowly, "you're a funny boy."

"Brainy, good-looking *and* funny! Are you sure you're feeling all right?"

"I mean, no one knows what you're really like."

"No one knows what anyone's really like, do they?"

The breeze blew a strand of hair into her mouth. "Very philosophical."

She pulled the strand out and tucked it behind her ear, and tried again, ponderously but not impatiently. "Do you remember the auditions for the play, when I came and asked you for your membership fee?"

"Of course."

"Well, we'd never met, had we? Except accidentally in corridors and so on."

"I knew who *you* were, though."

"Well, I knew who you were, too."

He put his head on one side and made a moron face. "Cle – ver!"

"Oh, shut up." For an instant, she did look impatient. She moved her leg away from his. "Just be serious for a minute, will you?"

He straightened his face.

"Well," she went on, "when I hadn't met you I thought what everyone thinks about you. But I was wrong."

His heart sank. Was she about to tell him that he was, famously, a dork? He waited while she settled differently on the seat, with her arm along the backrest. "You're top in maths in our year, aren't you?"

"I suppose I am." What else could he say?

"Well, people – boys, mainly – are always saying how good you are at maths and how they wish they were. Me too, for that matter. I'm in bottom set."

"Rubbish!" said Harry in genuine disbelief. "All they care about is how useless I am at football, not how good I am at maths!"

"No, *that's* rubbish. Even the real dumbos have worked out that there's no football exam."

He still couldn't believe her. "But – but..."

"Harry, listen." She put her hand on his thigh. Then she took it off again. "Before I met you, the only thing I knew about you was that people wanted to be friends with you but *you wouldn't let them.* You've got a reputation for stand-offishness, which people put down to the fact that you feel superior."

He was astonished. "But I don't!"

"I know that, and so does everyone who's got to know you through the play. Patsy and I were amazed when you turned out to be so easy to get on with, and funny, and – just *nice.* I mean, why do you think I'm sitting here with you today, freezing to death?"

She blew into her cupped hands. Neither she nor Harry spoke. He didn't know if he felt happy or not.

"Perhaps in searching for Fox's weak spot," she said, "you could remember that he's probably jealous of you."

She smiled one of her studied smiles, and shook back her hair. Harry felt as if she'd given him a telling-off he didn't deserve.

"But— "

She put up her palm to stop his protest. "No, don't say another word about it. I'm getting cold, and I want my tea. And I wouldn't say no to one of your chocolate mints, if there are any on offer. Let's go home, shall we?"

MASTER CLASS

"I hope you know what you're doing," said Louise as she and Harry left Miss Drew's room at lunchtime the next day.

Miss Drew had joyfully accepted the idea of a master class, and arranged it more readily than Harry was prepared for. "This Friday, after school?" she'd suggested. "Put 'all welcome' on the posters, Harry. This might be quite an event!"

"It was your idea, Miss Harding," he said.

"Abominable! Despicable untruth!"

It was a line from the play. Harry laughed. "Not about Simon, but about having a master class in the first place."

"Not with a *quadriplegic,* for God's sake."

"Don't call him that. He's just a man, like any other man."

"Not *quite* like any other man, Harry."

They went down the stairs and crossed the yard to the dining room. Harry glanced at his watch. If there were still enough late-finishers hanging around, he and Louise would be able to sit together without it being obvious. With hope in his heart he pushed the swing door and watched the sway of her skirt as she walked in ahead of him.

To his amazement, a shout went up. A loud, discordant buzz of approval. He heard Louise laugh with delight and saw her put her hand over her mouth.

Embarrassment checked the grin his lips wanted to make. "Shut *up*." He plopped his sandwich box on the table and sat down. "Load of idiots."

A crowd of Year Tens, and some Elevens, including Mig and Stolz, were at the table. Louise sat down and took a packet of crispbreads demurely from her bag.

"Mm ... cottage cheese and lettuce!" drooled Mig at her shoulder. "Got a bite for me?"

He came round the table and sat next to Harry. "What have you got, mate?"

Harry tore the corner off a ham sandwich and handed it over. "The amount you eat, Mig, you should be as huge as Stolz."

"I heard that, Pritchard," said Stolz from the end of the table. Louise, who had been joined by the dark-haired girl who played the maidservant, smiled secretively.

Mig watched the two girls for a few moments, trying to look brooding and magnificent, though neither of them were looking at him. Then he dropped a bombshell.

"What happened on Thursday, then, Harry?"

"What?"

"When you got in from Tonio's. *Did* they ground you for a fortnight?"

Louise was looking at Harry as if she could scarcely bear to. He swallowed. "Oh, no. They didn't do much, really."

Once Mig had started, he seemed to be on a roller-coaster. "You looked pretty rough by then, you know. You should have seen him!" he announced to the whole table. Then he turned back to Harry. "You got worse and worse all evening, mate. Tonio and Maggie were really worried about you. Why did you stay there so long?"

Louise put the crispbread back in its paper. A blob of cottage cheese lay on the table. She put her finger in it. She wasn't concentrating on what she was doing. But on her face Harry didn't see the dazzled look Simon had predicted. He saw horror.

"You didn't *go,* did you?" she said faintly. "Patsy said—"

"Go where?" asked the maidservant. "What's happened?"

To Harry's relief Louise looked down, wiping the cheese from her fingers with a tissue, swinging her hair over her confusion. "It's all right, Rebecca," she said in her clear voice. "It's a misunderstanding."

"What's all this, then?" Mig had scented scandal.

"Louise, this is Mig," said Harry before Mig could take a breath. "He was a good friend to me on Thursday night. He took me home in a taxi."

"Were you drunk?" asked Rebecca, eyes wide.

"No, he was ill," said Louise.

"Were *you* there too?" Eyes wider still.

"No," said Louise steadily. She was looking at Harry with a look that stripped him of his blazer, shirt and tie, flesh and bone. She could see his heart laid bare. "But I know he was ill. It was the day he and Gerard Fox had that fight. No one in their right mind would drag themselves in that state to a *restaurant*."

There was a bewildered pause.

"He was probably just trying to be a hero," Rebecca told Louise, with authority. "Boys are stupid like that sometimes."

The bell rang. During the din made by chairs scraping the floor Harry crammed the rest of his sandwich into his mouth and shut the lid of the box. His pride was punctured, but not completely deflated. And as Simon had predicted, Louise had excused herself.

He knew he should leave it there. He should let her be punished by her own guilt. He watched her pick up her bag and put the strap over her shoulder, pulling out some hair which had got trapped underneath it. He watched her push in her chair neatly and turn to go.

"Why didn't you phone me?"

It was a sharp whisper, loud enough for her to hear through all the other noise. Her head jerked round. She was near to tears.

"Look, Harry— "

"You said you'd be there."

"I said I was there most Thursdays."

"You said you'd *be* there."

She tried again. He could tell she wasn't acting. "It wasn't a firm arrangement. I didn't know if you'd come. We hadn't set a time, had we? If I'd phoned it would have made it into a – well, a *date*. Which it wasn't. I didn't want you to think I was – oh, never mind."

Her usual serenity had vanished. She put her hand to her throat. The second bell rang.

"Why did you phone me yesterday, then?" he persisted. It was surprisingly easy to ignore her distress. "You didn't need to do that, or to come round and deliver a present you could just as easily have given me today. So was that a *date*, or not?"

She wouldn't give in, though he could see tears glistening at the corners of her eyes. She tossed back her hair and looked at him in her actress way, head up, eyelids lowered, cheekbones in evidence.

"See you at a quarter to four, Malcontent," she said, and made for the door.

Frustration made him brave. "Don't count on it, Belladonna."

"Books-down, remember!" she said, without turning round.

Brig Fox turned up to Simon's master class.

When he saw him Harry felt as if someone had punched, or possibly stabbed, him in the solar plexus. A thousand reasons to feel uneasy jostled for space in his head. It was obvious Brig hadn't come because of any interest in acting. He must have come to goggle at the source of his triumph over Harry. He'd come to see the monkey man.

Panic-stricken, Harry searched the crowd of faces for the three henchmen. They weren't there. Brig was on a lone mission. The familiar feeling of helplessness threatened, but he fought it off. After all, Miss Drew had insisted he put ALL WELCOME on the posters. Brig had every right to be sitting there between the sound engineer's assistant and a younger boy Harry didn't know.

He'd had no trouble from him recently. Fox had lain low all week, unwilling to alert teachers to his activities after such a narrow escape. Harry predicted that he'd wait at least another week, until Harry's injuries had healed. Then he would devise a new indignity for him.

Unless Harry devised one for him first, of course.

Louise had been cool to him, too, since Mig's revelation. From where he sat in the second row he could see her profile, half-obscured by Patsy's sunburst of hair. She looked the same as usual, her face impassive, her legs casually crossed. She knew he was there but she didn't look at him.

Dad had brought Simon in his estate car with the wheelchair in the baggage compartment, its wheels in the air, looking like a huge beetle struggling helplessly on its back. Simon's cushions and water bottle had been piled beside it, and Simon himself had been lifted out of the car in Dad's arms.

It had been a comical sight. Simon was used to being carried by men – usually nurses or ambulance drivers, not sales managers, he had informed Harry cheerfully. But Dad wasn't used to carrying the six-foot tall, though very light, frame of a man twenty years his senior. His face had been a mixture of reverence, strain and embarrassment.

Harry had hardly been able to look. He knew that if Dad or Miss Drew or anyone else started to talk to Simon as if, in Simon's own words, he was deaf or mental, he would fall on his knees, right there in the car park, beating his chest and screeching in anguish. He'd waited by the car door, nervous as he had never been before.

"Are you OK?" he'd asked as Dad lowered Simon's fragile limbs into the chair.

"Of course I am, boy. Do you think I've never been out of the house before?"

Harry had hoped Simon wouldn't call him "boy" once they got into the school hall.

"Are *you* OK, Harry?" Dad had asked him. "You look a bit white. Nerves?"

"I suppose so."

"Don't worry. I'm sure Mr Schofield knows what he's doing." He'd thumped Harry gently on the shoulder. "I'll be back at five o'clock. Enjoy yourself, now."

Miss Drew had given Simon an ecstatic greeting, and introduced him to Mr Mitchell, who for some reason had turned up too. They had chatted to Simon for a few minutes, then Mr Mitchell had taken a chair to the back of the hall and sat down, planting his feet half a metre apart and folding his arms sturdily like a footballer in an old-fashioned photograph. Catching Harry's eye, he'd nodded to him and Harry had nodded back.

And now Simon's audience awaited his entrance. Every pore in Harry's skin seemed to be sweating. His school tie was strangling him. Have faith, he told himself. If *you* don't believe in Simon, who will?

Miss Drew introduced Simon as Mr Simon Schofield, a professional actor, and positioned the wheelchair where he requested. In front of the audience, on the floor not the stage. Then she sat down in the front row, looking flustered and keen.

"Miss Drew," said Simon unexpectedly. "Could I make a request?"

"Of course." Miss Drew got up, ready to do whatever he asked.

"Could you, and everyone else, call me Simon?"

She sat down again and bowed her head in her graceful way. "By all means. Simon."

There were some snorts of suppressed laughter. Harry saw a flash in Simon's eyes. "And now I have another request. Which of you gentlemen is Mr Fox?"

How did he know? *How?* Was it a lucky guess? Had he seen Fox somewhere before? Had Harry somehow given away the presence of his tormentor? Baffled, he waited.

Fox, his pointy face tense with suspicion, raised his hand. "Here, sir."

"Simon," said Simon.

Fox said nothing.

"Would you favour me with your company, Mr Fox?"

Fox's suspicion increased. He looked at Miss Drew, who nodded encouragement. As warily as a deprived child offered its first piece of chocolate, he got up and stood beside Simon's chair. Harry's heart began to use his injured ribs as a punchbag.

"May I call you Gerard?" asked Simon conversationally.

"How do you know my name?" Fox was using the polite voice he reserved for teachers.

"I know your mother, dear boy."

Everyone, even Miss Drew, smiled at the sight of Fox being called dear boy. Harry only just conquered the desire to turn round and look at Mr Mitchell's reaction.

"And you look just like her," said Simon, "though of course you have more hair on your upper lip."

The more intelligent members of the audience grasped the two-edged sword Simon had brandished, and a murmur went round. Fox, who was also intelligent, understood that his mother may or may not have been insulted. In the face of such ambiguity he was powerless. His nostrils flared in a way familiar to Harry, but he betrayed no other sign of emotion.

"Now, Gerard, would you please bring your chair and sit here by me?" asked Simon.

Fox did so. Then Simon ordered the boy who had been sitting next to Fox to bring his chair and sit on the other side of the wheelchair. Scarlet-faced, he obeyed. Next, the sound engineer's assistant was asked to bring his chair and sit beside Fox. And so on, until everyone, including Miss Drew, was in a circle.

"Now we can have a master class!" declared Simon.

The circle consisted of about twenty-five people. The cast of the play were all there. Louise and Patsy sat together as usual, almost directly opposite Simon. The other dark-haired girl, Rebecca, sat beside Patsy, with two more girls beside her.

MAESTRO, *a middle-of-the-road musician,* whose name Harry now knew was Jack Tillotson, and Craig Barrett, who played STORTELLI, *a nobleman of Pasta,* who was Belladonna's beau, were there too. They sat beside each other, lounging with their feet stuck out and their hands in their trouser pockets, being stars. Other actors like Harry were littered among the stage hands and technicians. Brig Fox was the only person there who wasn't a member of the Drama Club.

His bravery in turning up like this was astounding. Despite everything, Harry was impressed. A thought which he'd tried to stop himself thinking several times in the past week strayed into his mind again. If only Brig weren't such a twisted, small-minded bully, he might be a good person to have around.

Simon began to talk about the play. Harry allowed his attention to loosen, and watched the circle of faces. Some were looking at Simon, some were not. Some were rapt, others looked expressionless or bored. He steadied his nerve and glanced furtively at Louise.

She was sitting at a three-quarter angle, her legs crossed at the knees. Under her skirt he could see about two millimetres of white petticoat. One of her arms rested on the back of the chair, her fingers twisting her hair round and round. It was a habit he'd noticed before. Her body looked nice in her white school blouse and thin wool jumper. It went in and out at the right places, but was slight and, he knew for a fact, soft.

His reverie was disturbed by a movement. Patsy leaned across and whispered in Louise's ear. Without taking her eyes off Simon, Louise smiled knowingly, and whispered back. Then they looked at each other, and smiled again.

Girls, thought Harry. Always *rabbiting*. Always *plotting*.

His gaze travelled round the circle until it landed on Fox. He thought he'd be fidgeting, as he always was in class, or looking at the ceiling, rigid with boredom. But he wasn't. He was concentrating hard, looking straight ahead, with his arms folded. His face looked slightly flushed.

Harry looked at the place where Fox was looking. Then he looked back. Fox shifted, putting one grey-socked ankle up on the other knee. Harry noticed with a stab that his thighs had muscles in them – playing so much football must have had some pay-off – and his shoulders, hunched inside his blazer, were broader than the thin, angular ones

Harry had inherited from Mum.

Disbelieving, he followed Fox's gaze again. Patsy whispered to Louise, and shot an arrow-look at Fox. Louise, her eyes brighter than they'd been when Harry had looked at her a moment ago, twisted on her chair and let her hair fall over her cheek. Harry clutched the seat of his own chair, convinced for an anguished second that he was going to fall off it.

How could he have been so *stupid*? How could he have told Louise what an intelligent, potentially acceptable fellow Brig Fox was? She had actually said she thought Fox was good-looking! Why hadn't he burst into derisive laughter at this ridiculous notion? Why hadn't he assassinated Fox's character while he had the chance? What was the best way to kill himself?

"Right then, folks," Simon was saying, "I hope that's made some sense. Now, let's get down to some action. I want two boys and two girls."

No one volunteered.

"What are your names, Miss Brunette and Miss Redhead?" said Simon.

Harry knew that he had alighted on Louise and Patsy because they were sitting directly opposite him, and it was more difficult for him to see anyone else. They, of course, thought they'd been singled out for beauty and talent. Looking important, they announced their names and stood in the middle of the circle, awaiting further instructions.

The instructions, when they came, thrust a long,

sharp dagger into Harry's already dying self-esteem.

"What about you, Gerard?" said Simon. "You look a likely actor. Stand up. And you, Harry. Come and join the others."

Harry kept his eyes on Brig's face as they met the girls in the centre of the circle. It was pale, with a burning red smudge on each cheek. His eyes, which were very dark, had darkened further with embarrassment and excitement.

Simon described what he wanted them to do, but Harry hardly heard. His legs were weighted with invisible magnets. His eyes felt scratchy, as if he hadn't had enough sleep. Throughout the master class, wherever he stood or sat, whether he was involved in the action or not, some malevolent desire drew his gaze to Fox's face. And every time he looked at Fox, Fox's eyes were glued to the one thing in the room Harry couldn't bear them to look at.

He could have wept. Simon had insisted that Brig must have a weak spot, through which Harry could defeat him. But how could either of them have predicted that Brig's weakness – the one chink in the armour that defended him from every attack Harry might make – would be, of all things, Louise?

VILLAIN

Harry felt that he had made the ultimate sacrifice.

Well, perhaps not the ultimate sacrifice that history teachers meant when they talked about young men not much older than you being sent to unnamed graves. But it felt pretty ultimate to Harry.

Fox's desire for Louise was so obvious Harry wondered why he hadn't seen it before. And, he'd realized with a chill in his heart, *she* hadn't exactly run away from it. During the days following the master class, he'd catalogued the times he'd seen her in Fox's company. Not alone – Patsy and Rebecca were always there too – but on benches in the playground, at tables in the dining room and, lately, at rehearsals. Brig would be there, hanging around at the back of the hall, watching. And because he'd paid one pound fifty for the privilege, Miss Drew couldn't throw him out.

Reluctantly, Harry had begun to act coldly towards Louise. He knew he was risking losing her friendship altogether, but if that was the price of deliverance from Fox, he knew he was cowardly enough to pay it.

"Pritchard! Would you slow down a minute, for pity's sake?"

He turned. Patsy was grinning gleefully, her arms full of sheets of yellow, blue and pink paper. "Look, programmes!"

He grabbed the yellow one she offered him, and she stood beside him in the middle of the corridor and looked at a pink one. "Yellow for Tuesday, blue for Wednesday, pink for Thursday," she explained. "And tickets to match. Aren't they grand?"

Harry searched for his name. There it was, about halfway down the cast list. MALCONTENT, *a villain,* Henry Pritchard. It was real, then. It was happening.

Patsy's freckled fingers encircled his wrist as he tried to turn the page.

"And have you seen this? Miss Drew has roped in *Gerard Fox* as prompt! Now why d'you think she'd give one of the most important jobs to *him,* of all people?"

Harry looked at her, interested. Her face had turned into the exact colour of her hair.

"I mean, it's quite difficult, you know, Pritchard. Following the script in the dark."

"Why would he be in the dark?"

"Because he'll be sitting by the side of the stage, out of sight of the audience!" She was covering accidental confusion with deliberate impatience.

"And it's *dark* there, isn't it?"

Harry supposed that it was.

"He'll have a little torch, of course, and some light will spill off the stage," she explained. "But noticing when someone's forgotten their lines and isn't just pausing deliberately, and then prompting – just loud enough for them to hear without the audience hearing too – is really difficult."

"Well, Fox is pretty bright, you know," said Harry reasonably.

She stared at him. "That's what Louise says."

"There's more to him than meets the eye, Pats." At some stage during the past few weeks he had begun to copy other people and call Patsy, Pats. She didn't seem to mind, though she never called him anything but Pritchard. "Perhaps he's got hidden depths."

She gave him a mysterious look, and dug in her bag with her free hand. "Well, let's hope Miss Drew knows what she's doing. Here, take these tickets and sell them. Yellow for Tuesday, blue for Wednesday..."

"And pink for Thursday. I know. Can I keep this programme?"

"Sure you can. Take more, if you like. There's plenty."

He took another for himself and one for Simon.

"Try really hard to get rid of Tuesday's tickets, won't you?" she pleaded. "First night's going to be even worse if there's no one there to see it!"

Harry thought that maybe, on the whole, he

would prefer it if no one came on any of the nights.

"Costume fitting tonight," said Patsy. Her eyelids flicked down and then up again. "I hope you're wearing clean underpants."

He was accustomed by now to Patsy's attacks, and parried this one calmly. "Would you like to inspect them?" She was easy to tease and he couldn't resist doing it. "Pity the prompter doesn't need a costume."

Easy to tease. But she was on her guard now, and smiled amiably. "You're learning, Pritchard. See you later."

He folded the programmes and put them in his pocket. Then he watched Patsy's curly pony-tail until it turned the corner at the end of the corridor. So far, she had shown him wit, bravery, loyalty, friendship and good humour, as well as a lot more of the playfulness she'd subjected him to on that first day, when she'd squeezed his arm at the audition.

But Brig hadn't seen any of this.

Harry remembered Patsy's spluttering contempt for the whole Fox gang as she knelt beside him on the icy mud that nightmare day. Perhaps Dad was right about fickle females after all. They were allowed to change their minds, and decisive males were supposed to tolerate it with good grace.

It was difficult not to think "Girls!" in italics, though he tried hard. It was little short of incredible that Patsy should desire Brig's approval, but it was far less incredible that he remained unmoved by her admiration. Like Harry himself, Brig could only look at Louise.

Rehearsal had been called for half an hour's time, but Harry didn't want to join the others in the hall just yet. He didn't want to witness the nervous excitement as Patsy distributed tickets, and programmes were ripped open and names checked. And he didn't want to encounter the invisible screens Louise arranged around herself whenever she saw him these days. The misunderstanding about Tonio's had marked the beginning of her frostiness, but since Harry had made the decision to sacrifice his friendship with her to his fear of Fox, she had frozen into ice.

He went outside and sat on a bench in the playground. He didn't have his coat on, but the cold was bearable. The daffodils were out. The outlines of the beech trees along the border of the school field were beginning to blur again. Spring would come, and be followed by summer, and he and Dad and Emma would play cricket in the garden again. He uncrossed his legs and sat forward with his elbows on his knees, pushing his hair back with both hands.

Louise hadn't looked at him during the master class. Not even once. And when Simon had asked her to act something out with a boy, she had chosen Brig. She had actually caught him by the sleeve, deepening his already vermilion flush. And although Harry was quite well aware that she had done this for his personal torment, he was duly tormented.

After that, the Fox trap had fallen into place

with the speed and smoothness of a military manoeuvre. It had been easy for Harry to exploit Brig's weakness. It had been easy, given their obvious liking for each other, to engineer ways to bring him and Louise together.

Three times now, he'd succeeded. His masterpiece, when he'd pretended to have a sneezing fit so that Brig could read Malcontent's lines in a scene with Louise, had taken place at last night's rehearsal. He'd looked with satisfaction through streaming eyes at Louise's confusion and Brig's blush. But at the same time, he'd hated himself.

It was like playing chess with both the black and the white chessmen at the same time. He felt like God. And so far, Brig and his hangers-on *had* left him alone.

It had become such an obsession that one afternoon when Harry had taken Emma to buy some chocolate on the way home, he began to wonder if he had got kicked in the head after all.

"I want these," Emma had declared, picking up a box. "They're my favourites."

Not much interested, Harry had looked. Then, to Emma's surprise, he'd snatched the box out of her hand and put them back on the shelf. "You're not having those. Choose something else. And quickly, midget, or I'll go home without you."

The chocolates were called *Matchmakers.*

Sometimes he felt like Sydney Carton at the guillotine in *A Tale of Two Cities*, doing his far, far better thing. Sometimes he felt like Clark Kent, watching helplessly from behind his glasses while Lois Lane dreamed of Superman. Most of the time, though, he just felt awful.

And now, the first night of the play was only a week away.

Swinging on a trapeze had proved easier than Harry had feared. Mr Quigley had shown him how to leap off it on to the platform rigged up at the side of the stage, but didn't impart any information about how *he* had learned this in the first place. Harry couldn't imagine the stocky, middle-aged games teacher in white tights and sequinned epaulettes jumping neatly into the sawdust and going "Hup!" But he taught the technique well, and Harry knew he'd found his confidence. Tonight, though, he was going to have to do it in costume. Wearing a hat.

He pushed the door of the hall.

Miss Drew was standing in the middle of the stage clapping her hands for silence, her chin raised, her shoulders poised. He took the end seat in the second row. Brig, Patsy and Louise were sitting together in front of him. Brig's thigh, he noticed, was touching Louise's skirt.

Harry knew that Miss Drew had been to see Simon a couple of times since the master class. Simon, bemused by her interest in him but cheered by her enthusiasm, had given Harry edited reports. Tactfully edited, he suspected. After all, even their mutual regard for Simon couldn't make Miss Drew and Harry take off their badges saying Teacher and Boy.

"The costumes have arrived," she told them. "They're downstairs with your names on them. Boys under the stage, girls in the gym changing room. Put them on as quickly as you can and I'll inspect them."

Harry caught Patsy's eye. She used Louise's shoulder to smother a laugh.

"We're going to do the whole rehearsal in costume," said Miss Drew enthusiastically. "We've got to start doing the bowing and curtseying with the hats and skirts, or we'll never get it right. If anyone needs a safety pin, come to me."

In the room under the stage which Miss Drew always called the Green Room, though its walls were painted the same dirty beige as the rest of the building, Harry took Malcontent's clothes off the hanger.

Miss Drew had shown the boys already how to put on their ties, which were more like white cotton bandages than any tie Harry had ever seen. She'd told them to pull their shirt cuffs out of their coat sleeves, and to leave the top and bottom buttons of their waistcoats undone.

Harry did all this. But when he looked at his reflection he was unprepared for the transformation. He stared and stared, and craned his neck to look at his back view, and stared and stared again. Miss Drew had insisted that Malcontent must swagger, but he had always found this impossible in his school uniform. He experimented with a bit of swaggering now. It was impossible *not* to do it.

The high shirt collar pushed his chin up. The close-fitting tail coat forced his shoulders back and his chest out. The boots, which were riding boots lent by someone's dad who was a farmer, with the black breeches tucked inside them, seemed to elongate his legs and eliminate the skinniness of his thighs. Best of all was the high black hat and Susannah's riding crop.

"Good God, Pritchard!" said Jack Tillotson as he walked past, swaggering too. "*How* tall are you?"

The other boys had similar costumes, except Toady, the manservant, who wore a suit of livery. Their jackets were green and brown, their breeches tan, their waistcoats softly striped.

But Malcontent's clothes were all black, except for the gold-trimmed waistcoat and the white shirt, with its frilled cuffs hanging out of his sleeves. Once he'd got his side whiskers on, he knew he'd look unrecognizably villainous. He hoped that when Mum and Dad and Emma came to see the play on the last night, Emma wouldn't scream when she saw him.

There was a lot of prancing about and giggling, but Harry could see they were all pleased with their appearance. For the first time he began to understand the excitement Simon had known in his acting days. The satisfaction of wearing someone else's clothes and speaking with their voice, which Simon had so often experienced, was soon to be Harry's too.

If he could fight down his nerves and remember

the lines. And manage not to fall off the trapeze.

Summoned to the stage, he attacked the stairs as Malcontent, climbing them two and three at a time, his coat tails swishing round his legs. But when he got to the top, and heard screams of female laughter, reality tumbled back. He tried to push his stomach down into its proper place, knowing he had never felt so self-conscious, nor ever would again.

He took off the hat and held it with the whip in his right hand. He positioned himself behind Craig, who still had his hat on, and pretended to be adjusting his waistcoat. He couldn't look at Patsy, and he certainly couldn't look at Brig Fox. But the desire to look at Louise was stronger than his will. Slowly, so that no one would notice him doing it, he raised his head and looked.

By some inspired instinct, Miss Drew had got Belladonna a white dress. Low-necked, high-waisted, with puff sleeves like a little girl's party frock, it had a looped-up train which Louise held in her right hand. In her other hand she carried a white lace fan. She still looked like Louise, but what had happened to Harry when he'd put on his costume had evidently happened to her, too. The unaccustomed exposure of her chest was making her lower her shoulders and relax her arms. The long skirt made her look taller and more graceful. Her dark hair was flatteringly framed by a white bonnet, and a satin bow trembled under her chin. Her face was ablaze.

Six weeks ago Harry would have turned away,

disgusted by such a display of self-love. But today, in his black tailcoat and high boots, he was aware of his own, no less outrageous, vanity.

Patsy, as usual, broke the tension. "Sure these must have cost a fortune, miss!" she declared in her famous broad Irish. "Mother of God, have you robbed a bank or what?"

Miss Drew laughed affectionately. "Patsy O'Donnell, you're a born actress."

"Ha!" said Patsy to Louise, who laughed too. Then she turned back to Miss Drew. "Seriously though, miss. These lovely dresses. And the coats and breeches for these elegant gentlemen who used to be Beechwood boys! And the bonnets and fans and fob-watches and canes and everything else. Where did they come from?"

Miss Drew adjusted the ribbon of Patsy's bonnet, humming the first few bars of "Edelweiss". "They're from a professional company," she said. Her smile became more secretive. "I have my contacts, you know."

"But the *expense*!" insisted Patsy.

"They did cost a lot to hire, yes. That's why we haven't had them until today. But money is always forthcoming for worthwhile causes, you know."

As she turned from Patsy and went to inspect Rebecca's costume, Miss Drew flashed Harry one of her nanosecond looks. He met it fearlessly, wondering. She teased out the frills of Rebecca's maid's cap, not looking at him, and went on with

"Edelweiss".

Aware that his mouth had fallen open, he shut it, and looked away.

Susannah was lying on her stomach on the floor of the den, propped up on her elbows. "No, it's not 'is'. It's *'is't'*. I think," she said, frowning.

Harry sighed. "'*Is't* well that I am come'," he said for the fortieth time, "'and can bid you welcome again, my lady'. There, that's all I'm doing. Put the script away."

She rolled over and looked at him anxiously. "You don't know the lines, Harry, and there's only a week left. Hadn't we better go over them just once more?"

"No." His patience, which had been stretched between Susannah and the script for the last hour, had snapped. "I don't care if I forget it. Fox will just have to do his job properly and prompt me, won't he?"

"I suppose so," said Susannah. She had never heard of Fox. "But I thought I was helping you. Are you annoyed with me?"

He tried not to be hard on her. But the strain of being imprisoned with Susannah's brainless chatter in a small room while rain splashed against the window was becoming intolerable.

"Why don't we go downstairs and watch TV?" he suggested. Emma's company, for once, might come in useful.

"On Saturday morning?" She sat up and looked at her watch. "Won't Emma be watching children's programmes?"

"Well, we can watch children's programmes too." He snatched up the playscript and stuffed it into his schoolbag. "We're children, aren't we? Well, *you* are."

"Oh, Harry!" She was almost crying. "What's the matter with you?"

He knew, but couldn't tell her.

"Perhaps it's nerves," he said. "I've just had enough of the play for now, Suke, that's all. Give it a rest, will you?"

She took a tissue from her sleeve and wiped her nose. He was right, she was a child. She looked six years old again. Gawky, fair-haired, incongruously dressed in tight black jeans and a ribbed sweater, hauling herself from the floor to the old leather couch which Harry's dad insisted was good enough for the den.

"Sorry," he said, meaning it. "Look, do you want some coffee?"

Her face brightened. "Up here?"

"Up here."

"OK." She settled further into the couch. "Shall I get it?"

He smiled at her, feeling better. Her predictability reassured him that life would go on as usual, day after day, despite his own world's recent collapse. "No, you sit there."

When he got back with two mugs and a plate of biscuits on a tray, she had moved to the other, less sunken end of the sofa. She took the coffee but refused a biscuit.

"Come on," said Harry in exasperation. "Even supermodels have the occasional *snack*."

"Do you think I could be a supermodel?"

This wasn't the reaction he'd hoped for. He sighed. "Susannah, I don't know and I don't care. Just have a biscuit, will you?"

"Are you going to be horrible to me again?"

This was another echo from their childhood. Wincing inwardly, Harry knew that the only way to persuade Susannah was to flatter her. "You're slimmer than all the other girls already. And prettier," he added for good measure. "Now have a biscuit."

Predictably, she took one. "Do you really think I'm pretty?"

He tried to imagine Louise, or even Patsy, for all her boldness, saying something so obvious. "Of course I do." And then, to crush her, "You're as pretty as you were when you were six, which is more than can be said for most people."

She nibbled the edge of her biscuit, while Harry listened to the rain and wondered whether Simon was sitting at his window, watching the same rain fall on the immaculate garden. Tomorrow afternoon they would go enjoyably over the line-learning which had been such torture with Susannah.

"I know what I had to tell you." She gave him a suspicious look. "If you're listening."

He took two biscuits and dunked one in his

coffee. "I always listen to you because what you say is so interesting and informative."

She frowned unhappily. He longed with almost physical longing for her to turn into Louise, and laugh Louise's light, appreciative laugh. "Well, anyway. At Tonio's last night – where were *you*, by the way? – I was sitting with Mig and Stolz, and who do you think came in?"

"Who?" he asked obediently.

"Patsy O'Donnell and that stuck-up friend of hers, Louise Harrison."

"Harding," corrected Harry automatically, though his heart had performed a pole vault.

"Harding, then. I've never seen them in there before on a Friday night. And when I saw the boy they had with them, I was amazed."

"Why?" What new nonsense was this?

"Well, he was quite good-looking. Mig and Stolz knew him, but they were absolutely *horrible* to him, and would hardly even say hello. Patsy talked to Stolz a bit, then she went and sat at the table by the jukebox with Louise and this boy, who seemed to be Louise's boyfriend."

The table where Harry had sat for so long that night, *not* being Louise's boyfriend.

"What did he look like, this boy?" His heart had abandoned pole-vaulting in favour of diving, fast.

"Well, let's see. Dark hair, cut short. Not as tall as you, and sort of – " she paused, her biscuit in the air – "well-made. You know, not bony like most boys are."

Well-made enough to kick my ribs to pieces, thought Harry.

As Brig materialized in her imagination, Susannah got into her stride. "Nice dark eyes, sort of flashy. And expensive clothes. He had on one of those soft leather bomber jackets that cost *hundreds*."

Poor Patsy, he thought in despair. Brig's ability to attract girls seemed boundless.

"Do you know him?" asked Susannah. "I heard them call him Gerry."

Gerry? His despair deepened. "Yes, probably."

He couldn't tell her that dark-eyed, well-dressed "Gerry" was the originator of the blue-green smudge on his right eyebrow and the extensive scar tissue on his left knee.

"That Louise is a flirt. I bet she'd go out with anything in trousers," she said moodily. "And as for Patsy O'Donnell – you should have seen what a short skirt she was wearing! I got Stolz to take me home. I couldn't stand the spectacle any longer."

Harry's mortification seemed complete. His body seemed to have sunk so deeply into the uncomfortable end of the sofa that it would never get out again.

"Are you all right?" asked Susannah. She stood up and adjusted the waistband of her jeans. "You look a bit fed up."

"Me? Fed up? How could I be fed up when you are near?"

"Oh, don't start that again!"

At least she'd realized it was a joke. She took his

empty mug out of his hand and put it back on the tray. He watched her walk across the room, knowing that she knew he was watching her.

He fought against the instinct which told him that what he was about to do would mean the end of human life as we know it. But he had ruined every chance he'd ever had of going out, properly, with Louise. Patsy, who flirted with all the boys, only wanted Fox. So in the end, despite a lifetime spent trying to escape from her, Harry was left with Susannah.

"Why don't we go out tonight?"

It was the first time he'd ever said this to her.

"You and I?" She was suspicious.

His palms felt clammy. "Well, yes."

"Actually, Harry – " she swallowed nervously. "Thanks for asking me, but I'm going out with Stolz tonight. We're going to speedway."

He had to suppress a strong desire to laugh. At the impossible pairing of Stolz and Susannah, and at himself.

"Oh. So things are on between you and Stolz, are they?"

She flushed. She did look pretty. "Yes, I suppose they are."

He let his head fall backwards against the couch. What did it matter that Susannah should abandon him, since everyone else had? Nothing mattered now.

Except the play, of course.

FIRST NIGHT

Harry spent every spare minute of that last week at Simon's house. He even started having supper there, and staying until Nurse Margaret came to put Simon to bed at ten o'clock.

Mrs Driver, Simon's housekeeper, confided that she didn't understand why Simon hadn't gone mad years ago, confined to one room, with an outing to the day centre once a week. Yet he flatly refused to go on any of the trips organized by local charities to theme parks or the seaside.

"Last Christmas," she said one evening, as Harry helped her dry the dishes, "he wouldn't even go to the pantomime. 'Why don't you take us to see something fit for grown-ups for a change?' he said to them. He was really quite rude, telling them they treat disabled people like retarded children. Hang up my apron for me, Harry, there's a love."

He began to understand why Simon's eyes had filled with tears when he'd asked him to do the master class. He thought back to that first, unnerving visit to the white room. How long had it taken him to recognize how special Simon was? Five minutes? Perhaps less. So why couldn't everyone else see it too?

"How can I make people understand – you know, about Simon?" he asked.

"Well, you can start by arranging another master class for him to do," said Mrs Driver. "I've worked for him for ten years, and I've never seen him as happy as he was that night."

All week he and Simon worked on his lines, and they looked at Simon's old reviews, and they talked endlessly about the play. But Harry couldn't bring up the subject of the Fox trap.

Sometimes he would look intently at Simon when Simon was looking at the playscript, willing him to say, casually, "What happened about Brigadier Gerard, and the lovely Louise?"

He wished that his heart could open like a box, and Simon could take out the regret that lurked there, and the guilt, and the self-loathing. He had been carrying them around for a long time, and they were getting heavier and heavier. He was sure that Simon would know a place where he could abandon them, if only he could explain. But Simon never mentioned it.

And all the time, day after day, Harry's fear grew. On the last Sunday before the play opened he couldn't concentrate on anything, and Simon said he must be either drunk or in love.

"If only!" he said, with feeling. "But it's neither

of those, Simon. I'm just scared stiff."

"Of course you are. I always was too." They were playing chess. "Are you going to make this move tonight, or wait until I'm dead and you're senile?"

"What did you used to do, to calm yourself?"

Simon looked at him shrewdly across the chessboard. "Stand up, boy."

"Don't call me boy."

"I'll call you whatever I like. Stand up."

Harry stood up.

"Now, where's your weight?" asked Simon briskly.

"What?"

"You heard. What do you weigh? About ten stone?"

"Nine stone eleven."

"Well, nine stone eleven doesn't float about like ectoplasm. It's got to settle somewhere, and when you're on stage you have to know *precisely* where it is."

Harry experimented. He put the nine stone eleven over his right foot then his left, then back again. Then he divided it between them.

"It's over both my feet, I think."

"Good. That's where it should be, when you're standing still. And when you move, remember it's torso first, legs next. Leading with the legs needs perfect balance and is best left to dancers, as I'm sure Elizabeth has told you."

Elizabeth was Miss Drew.

"But what's this got to do with feeling nervous?"

"In controlling your body, you control your nerves," said Simon simply. "You have power over *them,* not the other way round."

Harry tried a few more positions, centering his weight over his feet after every change. "But you can still forget your lines, can't you?" he asked apprehensively. "Just before I go on my mind goes blank."

"Oh, that's quite normal. But a few relaxation exercises will help deal with stage fright, if you learn them properly. Copy what I do."

Simon taught him to breathe deeply, all the way from his diaphragm, and release the breath through his nose. He showed him how to exercise his neck muscles and warm up his voice like a singer. Harry's panic shrank, but only slightly. "Is this what real actors do?"

"Of course. And sometimes they go to the pub and have three glasses of brandy, but I won't recommend that for fear of what your dear mother might say."

On Monday they had the dress rehearsal. Harry remembered all of Malcontent's words, more or less accurately, but a door stuck when he tried to open it and he was late for an entrance. Miss Drew screamed that it was a *dance,* you stupid boy, and if you missed a step the whole thing collapsed. Pale with exhaustion, Patsy suggested calmly that the door had expanded because the weather was damp, and Miss Drew apologized to Harry afterwards.

That night Harry slept. He slept as if someone

had given him pills, or knocked him unconscious. When Mum came in with his tea he couldn't believe it was daylight. He dozed during Tuesday morning's lessons, his stomach rolled up as tightly as a frightened hedgehog, and tried to forget about the play. But when he got home at half past one, the cast having been given the afternoon off, he found he couldn't sleep at all.

He practised his lines. Then he watched an ancient black and white movie on TV. Then he picked up Emma from school and made her tea and toast. Then he phoned Simon.

"Can't you come tonight?" He'd decided, suddenly, that he wanted Simon there.

"I'm coming on Thursday, with your parents and Emma. We arranged it."

"Can't you come tonight as well?"

"I haven't got a ticket."

"You don't need one. You're part of the play, not the audience."

"I fully intend to be part of the audience on Thursday. And I don't want to see the play till then. Now calm down and get off the line. I'm expecting another call."

Harry was sure he wasn't. "I can't calm down."

"Do the breathing exercises I taught you. Have a bath. You know the drill. Now get off the line."

"Aren't you going to say good luck?"

"Certainly not. That's bad luck. Phone me tomorrow. Goodbye, now."

At six o'clock Mum drove him to school. She

didn't say good luck either. She said what she and Dad always said. "Enjoy yourself, now."

Harry sat numbly in the dressing-room, watching the others arrive and start to put make-up on, and chat to each other. They greeted him, and asked if he was OK, and he said he was. But his body felt inert, weighed down by apprehension.

It was all right for them. Jack and Craig and the others had all been in plays before. And they were the show-off types who must have learned long ago to trade nerves for glory. But he didn't know how to do that. He would never know what glory was.

All he knew was how ill he felt, and how likely he was to be sick.

"Half an hour, boys!" Miss Drew opened the door. When she saw Harry her face changed. "Malcontent! Get dressed, will you? And who's doing your make-up? And where are your whiskers?"

"I feel ill," he confessed faintly.

She took his costume off the rail and threw it against his chest. "Well, so does everyone else. Be your age, Pritchard."

Silence had fallen in the dressing-room. She'd never called him Pritchard before. "Do you want to ruin it for everyone?" she demanded. "You're on first, so get dressed *now*."

He didn't move, and no one spoke.

"*Harry!*" She had begun to wail. "Pull yourself together and make a start, will you?" She tossed her hair back ineffectually. Her eyes looked a bit wild. "Here, Gerard, help him." She grabbed Fox, who had just appeared in the doorway. He was wearing the leather jacket which Susannah had so admired. "Harry's got to be ready in twenty minutes. I'll be in the girls' dressing-room if you want me."

Fox glared down at him, his eyes glittering. The insane notion came to Harry that he should change places with him. He was sure that Fox would be a superlative villain and he himself would be the best prompt ever to grace the prompt corner. He had never hated Fox more.

"Piss off, Fox," he said.

He hated him for his persecution over so many months. He hated himself because he'd given up Louise, without any sort of fight, in order to end that persecution. Most of all, he hated him for being intelligent enough and good-looking enough for Louise and Patsy – and Susannah too, for pity's sake, who had never even spoken to him – to chalk him up as desirable.

"Put your costume on." The reasonable voice. The plausible-liar voice.

"Don't tell *me* what to do, bum-brain."

Craig Barrett, who was an Upper Sixth Former and Deputy Head Boy and Louise's leading man, intervened.

"For God's sake, you two! Are you trying to start another fight?" He began to take Harry's costume off the hanger. "Fox, clear out and go and sit in the prompt corner. Here's your shirt, Pritchard. Now put it on and I'll do your tie. Goodbye, Fox."

But Fox didn't move. His toothpaste

advertisement teeth were showing, though he wasn't quite smiling. His fists were clenched inside the pockets of the bomber jacket. He kept shifting from one foot to the other.

Harry's misery had deepened. Watched by Fox, half hidden behind the costume rail, he put the shirt on, and the waistcoat and breeches, and then the boots. Craig sat him down and began to smear make-up on his face. "Where's the glue for your whiskers?"

Harry knew what Fox was doing. But he could no longer push Harry's head down the toilet or throw stones. They were each beholden to their unspoken truce. He hated Harry as much as Harry hated him. And if this was the battle of wits Simon had foreseen, Harry was no longer interested in winning it.

Craig tied his tie, then Harry put on his jacket and fumbled the buttons into their holes. When Malcontent stood before the mirror once again, his shaking fingers closed around the riding crop and the brim of the black hat.

"Five minutes!" Miss Drew's head came round the door again. "Line up for inspection!"

They did so, except Fox. He had withdrawn further into his hiding place, and Miss Drew didn't notice him. She adjusted a few ties and rubbed in some smudges of make-up, her face alight with relief. They were all there, they were all dressed. They were all, suddenly, her darlings. She clasped her hands and bit her lip, like a little girl with a birthday present. "Don't let me down, boys."

And then there was no more time.

Malcontent's first entrance was from the prompt side. The stage was blacked out and it was very dark in the wings. Fox sat down in the prompt corner and flicked on the torch. He held it down on the first page of the script, and its beam spread out, underlighting his face with a mysterious greenish glow.

Suddenly, Harry's stage fright was obliterated by another, different fear. It took hold of his legs and shook them violently. He recognized it as the fear he'd felt so many times when Fox's familiar footsteps and nasal voice had sounded behind him in the corridor. Now, as he stood trembling in the darkness, it had become distilled into a purer form. Fox's hatred was almost palpable.

Miss Drew signalled to him from the other side of the stage. She couldn't hear his galloping heart or see the sweat which was seeping through his make-up. Trying to breathe, he stepped on to the stage. He could only just see his white cross, but he found it and stood on it.

He planted his feet with his weight squarely above them, as Simon had taught him. He raised his chin and lowered his shoulders, and prepared to sweep the floor with his hat in the exaggerated bow he'd practised every night for a week in the white room.

The hubbub in the hall died. The curtains opened and Harry's spotlight came on. Blinded, he took off his hat and bowed.

The bow was received with giggles and scattered

clapping. But as Harry performed it and launched into the opening lines his fear evaporated.

"Lady – beware! Put up your fan;
Before you stands a desperate man..."

His voice sounded low-pitched, but assertive, as if it was no longer his voice at all. Suddenly, he knew that Fox's power over him ended where the spotlight began.

It was like a fog clearing. Standing beside Fox in the darkness, he had felt a vast, overwhelming fear. But now, as he left the stage on the other side and Jack Tillotson gave him a thumbs-up sign, understanding the fear seemed ridiculously easy.

He's probably jealous of you, Louise had said.

Harry's reputation for remoteness had set him apart as decisively as his maths marks. It seemed obvious now. But it hit him with a stab that if it had been obvious six months ago, when he and Fox first got put in the same sets for maths and physics, he would have made a superhuman effort to make friends with him. He was pretty sure he'd have liked him. And Fox would have liked Harry, too. But it was too late now, and fear had been quick to fill the space which Harry's ignorance had left empty.

It's *you* who thinks you're a dork, Simon had said.

The truth of this had crushed him when he first heard it, and crushed him again now as he leaned against the wall, his hat and whip in his hand. He wasn't on for another twenty minutes, and knew he should go back to the dressing room. But he didn't want to. He wanted to stay near the place where Malcontent came alive.

There was a rustling sound behind him, and he looked round. Louise, in her white dress and bonnet, with the lace fan in her hand, had come into the wings to wait for her first entrance. She looked at him. Then, unexpectedly, she smiled.

"I hear they liked you," she whispered.

"Well, they're bound to like *you*."

"Shut up!" hissed Miss Drew.

Louise's smile stayed in his imagination after she'd gone on. He watched her doing the scene, kicking the train of the dress out of the way, curtseying low to Craig, flicking open and fluttering the fan. The audience would think she was lovely. She *was* lovely.

When they came off, she and Craig looked sweaty and excited. "They *laughed*!" she whispered to Miss Drew.

"Of course they did. Harry, get behind the door. You're on in three lines."

He was on stage for a long time, though he didn't have much to say. From where he stood he could just see the light on Brig's face. No one had forgotten their words yet, but Brig had to keep his head down, following the script, and couldn't look at Harry.

Understanding the fear was one thing. But dealing with it was something else. What did Malcontent use to overpower his victims? He flattered and fawned over people, while secretly plotting revenge on them.

He kept his nerve and didn't allow anything to get in the way of his ambition. He was strong.

And how had Simon survived for thirty years, immobilized, imprisoned? He seemed to be able to deal with everything, no matter how complicated. He was strong too, in his head.

Why had Louise smiled at him? Because she was strong enough not to carry her private feelings into the wings on the first night? Of course she was. She knew the play was more important than her off-stage troubles. And Patsy's strength was so obvious that a child younger than Emma could see it.

Well, he could be strong too. And he would use his strength to conquer his fear of Fox. He would be strong enough to do what he should have done six months ago. Like Malcontent, he would make his enemy his friend.

When Harry climbed the platform at the side of the stage and grasped the trapeze rope, he felt like a cartoon hero. He felt invincible. He felt as if he could climb Everest. Now, before bedtime.

Far below, Fox's dark head was silhouetted against the torchlight. Its distorted shadow spread over the wall like a stain. Harry pushed his hat tightly on to his head and positioned the trapeze bar. He was extremely hot, and his side-whiskers were getting itchy. But nothing could diminish the power which Malcontent had given him.

He heard his cue. He pushed off with his feet and swung out across the stage, the air whistling in his ears. He remembered the "is't" on "Is't well that I am come, my lady". But the line was drowned.

Everyone involved with the play had got used to the trapeze, having seen him swinging on it so often, badly, then better and better. But the audience was unprepared. They gasped, and then screamed.

That's what farce does, Miss Drew had told them. Farce makes the audience scream. If we hear that scream, we'll know we've done it.

The difficult sequence with the trapeze, the opening and shutting of doors, the final unravelling of the misunderstanding – the most complicated scene in the play, which Harry and Patsy and Rebecca and Jack had worked on until nine o'clock last night – ticked past like clockwork. The audience screamed and screamed, and when Harry approached the front of the stage, snarling and spitting Malcontent's poison, he saw more than one person put their hands over their eyes, or their mouths, or hide their faces altogether.

It was magic. Simon always insisted that theatre was a form of magic, but Harry had never really understood. He'd assumed Simon's memory was tainted with time and longing, and saw magic where magic couldn't be. But as he raised his hat and strode off, beating his whip against the top of his boot, the applause was so loud that he thought the sound crew must have somehow amplified it. And when he got to the wings it went on so long that Craig and Louise's final brief scene had to wait.

Miss Drew, who didn't seem to mind his sweaty shirt and sticky make-up, put her thin, muscular arms around his chest and hugged him tightly.

Badges didn't matter tonight. He was an actor. He had taken on something he didn't think he could do, and had done it.

"Bravo, Harry," she whispered as Craig pulled Louise on to the stage. "Simon's in the audience, you know."

He stood back and stared at her.

"He didn't want me to tell you, but I think it's all right to do so now."

"But..."

"Shush now. Get ready to take your bow. Remember to take your hat off before you go down. Go on."

He stood in the line with the others while they bowed and curtseyed. Then Craig, unrehearsed, poked him in the back and he stepped forward. The noise level grew. Harry bowed boldly. As his head came up he saw Simon's wheelchair at the end of the back row.

His heart full, he saluted him.

In the dressing-room the noise was scarcely less raucous than it had been in the hall. But above it Harry heard his name being called.

It was Jack. "Mitchell's in the corridor, asking for you. I invited him in here, but he won't come."

"Mitchell?" He was puzzled. "What does he want?"

Jack shrugged, and began to take off his make-up. "Why not go and find out?"

Mr Mitchell was waiting self-consciously by the door to the stage.

When he saw Harry he took a couple of steps

towards him and grasped his hand. "Congratulations, Pritchard."

"Thank you, sir." He looked down at his stained shirt and bare feet. "I was just getting changed."

"Well, I won't keep you. I just wanted to say," – he lowered his voice – "that it's the end of term on Friday. Remember what we agreed?"

"Yes, sir. But I won't have any more trouble from Fox. I've sorted him out."

Mr Mitchell looked interested. "And may I ask how?"

No, you may not. "I can't tell you, sir."

"Why not?"

"Because I can't tell you, sir."

Mr Mitchell looked at him thoughtfully for a moment. Then he nodded his head decisively. "Well, as long as it didn't involve bloodshed, I suppose it doesn't matter."

"It didn't, sir."

It involved Louise-shed. But how would Mr Mitchell ever be able to understand what *that* was?

"Off you go and get out of that costume, then. And well done again. I never knew you could act so well."

"Neither did I," confessed Harry. "But Simon Schofield's been a great help. And Miss Drew, of course."

Mr Mitchell smiled. This was such a rare occurrence Harry had to check a stare. "Yes, Elizabeth Drew – or E. E. Gibbard, dancer, actress and *playwright,* I believe," he said pointedly, "is a formidable lady. See you in maths tomorrow, Pritchard. Don't be late. Goodbye, now."

Harry's many astonishments of that evening disappeared under the enormity of this new one. He went back into the dressing-room and sat down. Fox was nowhere to be seen, and most of the cast had gone.

"Well done, Pritchard," said Craig good-naturedly as he packed his bag. Then he looked at him, frowning. "Are you all right?"

His eyes found Craig's face. He tried to look normal. "Oh, yes."

"It's all been a bit too much, tonight, hasn't it?" said Craig, with feeling. "Well, remember you've got to do it all again tomorrow. And Thursday!"

Harry nodded.

"There's a party on Thursday night after the performance. At Louise's house. The whole cast and crew are invited. You'll be there, won't you?"

He nodded again.

"See you tomorrow, then. Have a shower when you get in. You stink."

"So do you, Barrett," said Harry, removing more badges.

As Craig opened the dressing-room door, Brig Fox came through it and leaned against it. Harry took off his breeches and put on his jeans and sweatshirt. As he went to hang his jacket on the costume rail he passed Fox.

He had the protection of Toady, who was still combing his hair at the other end of the room.

Fox wouldn't risk a physical attack. But if Harry was ever going to approach Simon's level of courage, and make a mental attack on Fox, he knew he had to do it *now*.

"Coming to the cast party on Thursday, Brig?"

Fox's face changed. It seemed to blur round the edges, as if all its muscles had relaxed. This new face gazed at Harry for a second, then disappeared under deeply drawn eyebrows. "What's it to you?"

"You're in the crew, aren't you?" They eyed each other. "Well, Barrett says that all cast and crew are invited."

"Are you up to something, Pritchard?"

Harry put his foot up on a chair and took a long time to tie the laces of his trainers, so he wouldn't have to look at Fox's bewilderment. "Why do you always think people are up to something?"

"Are you trying to make a fool of me? I know you ratted on me to Mitchell."

Harry sighed. Here they were, back in the toilets with Harry's head in the bowl. "I didn't, but even if I had it wouldn't make any difference."

It was an effort to keep his voice light and reasonable. He changed his feet over and started on the other lace, concentrating on it as if it were the most important thing in the world. Toady hung up his suit of livery, said good night and left.

"What do you mean?" asked Brig suspiciously.

The moment had come. Harry's nerve staggered, but he propped it up. He'd brought the moment on himself, after all.

"What I mean is that what Mitchell knows, or who told him, doesn't matter any more." His breathing seemed very fast, and he tried to slow it down. "What matters is that we're here, the two of us, talking like civilized people. We've never done this before, have we?"

He couldn't see Brig's astonishment, but the space between them in the deserted dressing-room vibrated with it. He put his foot down and straightened up.

"*Why* haven't we done this before, Fox? Any ideas?"

He half-expected Brig to laugh, or to take a swing at him. But the bright, dark eyes and well-shaped lips were as serious as he had ever seen them, and the fists stayed in the pockets.

"You think you're really clever, don't you?" Fox's voice was cold, but it had lost the aggressive menace it had contained a few minutes ago. "You think you're so clever that no one's good enough to be your mate. But you're the stupidest, saddest no-hoper in the school."

Harry made himself think about Malcontent. He remembered something Simon had once said about him being the squash-wall off which all the other characters' malice bounced. Well, he could be a squash-wall too.

"You're right," he said, trying to check the trembling in his legs. "I am clever. But so are *you*. In fact, I'd always thought you'd be a good friend to have.

Then you started sticking my head down the toilet."

This wasn't strictly true, of course. Harry had never noticed the potential of Brig as a friend until Simon had made him do so. But that scarcely mattered now.

"What the hell are you talking about?" asked Brig urgently. He advanced on Harry, his fists clenched inside his pockets, his eyes narrowed. "What's all this stupid crap about *friends*?"

Harry's familiar Fox-fear threatened, but he beat it back. "Well, we've got things in common, haven't we?"

"Like what?"

Like Louise, he might have said. But that would be too ludicrously brave even for Malcontent. "Like you being top in physics and me being top in maths."

"Terrific!" said Fox, with contempt. "Do you want everyone who's top in their set to be 'friends', and play jolly games together, Pritchard?"

"Don't be such a moron."

The skin on Fox's pointy cheekbones stretched tighter. Harry swallowed. His throat was very dry, and all his muscles were tense. But he and Fox had come a long way on a dangerous road together. He couldn't turn back now.

"We both know why you came to that master class." His voice shook slightly on the last word. "And we both know why you're here, working on the play."

Fox's eyes glittered. He seemed to be having difficulty moving his mouth. "What are you talking about?"

"And I remember that poem you got a prize for when we were in Year Seven. You're not such a hooligan as you like to make out. And I'm not so – " what was Louise's word? – "so stand-offish as *I* like to make out."

Brig's eyes didn't leave Harry's face. They searched and searched it with a cold, wondering light. Inside, Harry battled with his instinctive distrust of Fox, his uncertainty about what to do next, and the depressing knowledge that he had driven the last nail into the coffin which contained his relationship with Louise.

He and Brig went on looking at each other. Harry waited, sweating.

Fox was sweating too. After what seemed years he wiped his upper lip with the back of his hand. "This party," he said in his familiar nasal voice, his breath coming down his nose fast, " ... all the girls are going, are they?"

"I expect so." He tried, but failed, to speak Louise's name. "Er ... Patsy and the others. You know."

Harry watched Fox's Adam's apple travel up and down his throat. His tension had relaxed a fraction. He zipped his jacket and ran his tongue around the inside of his mouth. "You're pathetic, Pritchard," he said. "You don't know what the hell's going on, do you?"

Without glancing again at Harry, he slipped away, silent in his soft backstage-crew shoes. When he'd gone Harry leaned against the dressing-table, exhausted. He looked at Malcontent's hat, propped on top of the rail, and, absurdly, punched the air.

"Why isn't there a *star* on this door!"

Louise was leaning on the door frame, her face shining with cold cream and happiness. She had changed into jeans and her white coat. "Have you seen Miss Drew?"

"Well, backstage. She gave me a hug."

"Did she? Let me hug you too, then!"

And before he could stop her, or even move, she had put her arms around his neck. As before, she felt small and slim and resilient, and smelled of make-up.

"We're all so proud of you," she said, standing back. "Are you coming to the party on Thursday night? I know it's at my own house, but will you – you know, take me?"

Harry felt as though he had walked into the wrong scene in the wrong play. He held her wrists, baffled. "But surely you want *Fox* to do that, not *me*?"

"What?" Her eyes widened. Then she gasped. "Oh, Harry!"

He dropped her wrists in disgust. "You sound like Susannah Gold."

She put her hand over her mouth. Above it, her eyes were laughing.

"What is it?" he asked.

"It's *Patsy* who'll be going with Gerry. She's – " – she saw Harry's expression – "Fox, I mean. She's liked him for ages."

Harry's brain seemed to have slowed down. "But he doesn't like *her,* does he?"

"Of course he does! It took some nerve to turn up at the master class like that, just because he fancied her, but you were right about Fox. There's more to him than meets the eye."

Harry's exhaustion became unbearable. He sat down and watched his foolishness unreel like a video in fast-forward. At the master class, while he had been suffering the worst torture Fox had ever inflicted on him, Fox had been looking at Patsy O'Donnell.

Unable to hold his head up any longer, he let it fall to the table and left it there among the screwed-up tissues and sticks of make-up. With no attempt at disguise, he groaned aloud. Then he thought about Emma and the chocolates, and groaned again.

Louise put her hand on the back of his head. He didn't move. "I'm a total and utter and complete dorkhead," he said. But he said it happily.

"Look at me, Harry." Her voice was serious. "I want to say something I should have said ages ago."

He raised his head, and she looked earnestly into his face. "You were right about that night when I didn't turn up at Tonio's. I should have made a definite arrangement."

"Oh, that's— "

"No, listen. I knew you'd been hurt in the fight. I should have phoned and asked how you were, at least."

She put her hand on the dressing table, close to his hand. "That's why I phoned on the Sunday, and came round with your present. But then, when we went for that walk and you were being so nice, I couldn't mention it. You must have thought I was so rude."

She paused, swallowing. Her little finger came up like an antenna and landed on the knuckle of his third finger. He looked down at it. It was much smaller than his. "And you tried to spare my feelings, didn't you? You didn't even tell me you went to meet me, and when I found out, I was horrible to you because I didn't know what else to do."

Her colour had risen. Her skin looked velvety and pink, like the sweet peas which Mum grew on the trellis at the bottom of the garden.

"No wonder you've been so cold with me for the last couple of weeks. I've deserved it. But let me apologize now, and we'll start again. If you want to."

"I want to."

"And will you take me to the party?"

"What do you think?"

They smiled at each other. Then Harry thought of something. "Is Simon invited to the party too?"

She tilted her chin towards his reflection in the mirror. It wasn't her actress tilt, though. "Of course, if you want him to come."

"I *do* want him to come. He *must* come."

"Why?" She met his eyes, alert.

"Because he hasn't been to a party for thirty

years. The last one he went to, on his motorbike, was the one he never arrived home from."

Her hand went to her mouth. She had never heard Simon's story.

"He must think about that party a great deal," said Harry, with feeling.

After a moment's pause, she put her third finger on his middle one.

"You're pretty fond of old Simon, aren't you?"

"Of course."

Her hand covered his. It felt light and, like the rest of her, soft. He grinned as a picture suddenly came into his mind. "I mean, without Simon, how could I have found out how interesting a monkey's life can be?"

She stared, mystified. Then understanding came into her eyes and she began to laugh. Harry's head felt as if it had taken flight. He laughed too.

And they were still laughing when they went outside, where Dad was waiting with the car to take Harry and Simon home.

THE BOY-FREE ZONE
Veronica Bennett

Living in the "boy-free zone" of a small town, Annabel is preparing for a long, dull summer. Then Sebastian appears... Seventeen, handsome, self-confident and American, Sebastian has the impact of a bombshell on Annabel and her friends. Passions run high and Annabel finds herself confronted by some alarming surprises. But most surprising of all is the discovery of the power that lies in her own hands...

"A teenage Jane Austen." *The Times*

"Entertaining and thoughtful." *The Irish Times*

FISH FEET
Veronica Bennett

Erik Shaw loves dancing and wants to audition for the Royal Ballet School. But that means making some tough decisions – such as giving up the Falcons football team and letting down old friends. Then there's Ruth, a fellow ballet dancer to whom Erik is becoming increasingly attracted. Can their relationship survive the rigours of practice and competition? And has Erik got the strength of will as well as the talent to achieve his goal?

READ MY LIPS
Jana Novotny Hunter

This deaf city war has been going on too long! It's time signers and speakers learned to get along.

Cat's had enough of the in-fighting at her school. So what if some students, like her, use sign language and others use speech? With the end of school looming, they're going to need all the help they can get to cope with the scary, hearing world of "outside". Which is why Cat decides to learn to speak again, despite her best friend's opposition. And when she falls for a speaker, she risks losing everything.

But Cat is determined that her voice will be heard...